ALSO BY JOE LOOBY

THE TENTH SERIES

The Tenth Trail Mark — *the story of the men who climbed.* A WWII Novel of Courage, Sacrifice, and the 10th Mountain Division.

The Tenth Station — *the story of the man who taught them how to fight.* A WWI Novel of Love, Courage, and the Rock of the Marne.

The Tenth Command — *the story of the men who led them.* A WWII Novel of Leadership, Redemption, and the 10th Mountain Division.

To my mother, Nancy Caroline Whitenack Looby

CONTENTS

AUTHOR'S NOTE

This novel is a work of historical fiction, inspired by the incredible true events of the Second Battle of the Marne in July 1918.

While the personal story of Price Hays has been imagined, the historical framework—and the astonishing bravery of the U.S. 3rd Infantry Division—is very real.

The heroic actions of First Lieutenant George "Price" Hays, whose Medal of Honor citation forms the heart of this story, serve as a powerful testament to the courage of that generation.

This book is my humble tribute to the soldiers who became known as "The Rock of the Marne" and to all the service members and their families who hold the line.

A NOTE ON THE EVE OF WAR

In 1914, as Europe descended into a war of machines and trenches, America remained a nation apart—protected by an ocean and a deep-seated tradition of isolationism. Its horse-and-buggy army was unprepared for the industrial-scale slaughter about to begin, a thought as foreign as the conflict itself.

Along the coast, rugged "storm warriors" of the U.S. Life-Saving Service still battled the sea with wooden boats, oars, and an unwavering code of honor, embodying an elemental American courage.

It was a world on the precipice—about to be swept away by the mechanized fury of modern war.

A Journey of War and Heart

This story follows Price Hays from the quiet grief of his youth in the Carolina Upstate to the crucible of the Western Front. The maps below trace the two key landscapes of his journey—the shores that shaped his character and the battlefield that forged his spirit.

Map 1: Sullivan's Island, 1914

This map depicts a fateful stretch of beach known as the Tenth Station, where a single act of courage would alter Price's life forever.

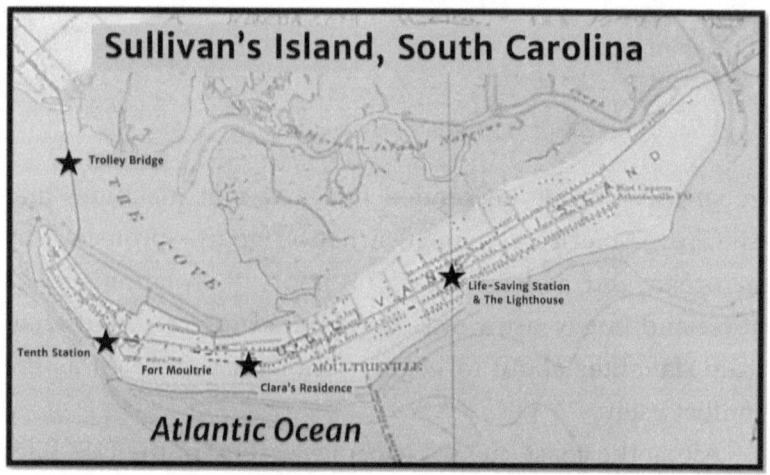

Map 2: The Western Front, 1918

This map shows the terrain where a lone soldier would undertake one of the Great War's most harrowing Medal of Honor actions—on one of history's darkest nights.

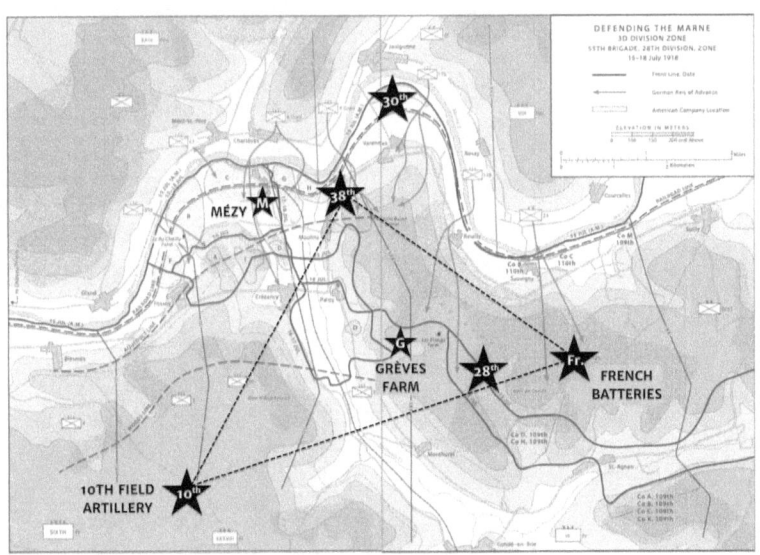

PART I: THE STATIONS

"The tide rises, the tide falls, The twilight darkens... ;"

— Henry Wadsworth Longfellow, "The Tide Rises, the Tide Falls"

1

THE RIVER - PART I

MAY 1914

Greenville, South Carolina

The shriek of the mill whistle was the first thing Price Hays heard every morning—a sound that sliced through the Carolina dawn and called the living to the mills along the Reedy River. Steam rose from the rooftops like ghosts of the night shift.

Seventeen-year-old Price and his mother lived in the shadow of the grand Presbyterian church where his father had once preached, but it was the whistle, not the church bells, that set the rhythm of their lives. Their home was a modest second-floor apartment, well kept, where the scent of his mother's cooking mingled with the lingering smell of timeworn books and his father's pipe tobacco.

His father had been a man of gentle wisdom—the center of their world—now gone, taken by a sudden heart attack that left a void as wide as the Carolina sky.

Greenville was a city caught between two worlds,

proudly calling itself the "Textile Center of the South," while the scent of pine and red clay still clung to its edges.

From the window, Price could see smoke rising from the stacks of the Camperdown and Brandon mills—hulking brick fortresses that hugged the river. His father, the late Reverend Hays, had once preached that the river was a source of life, but now it powered a new, insatiable god of textile and trade.

Down on the street, the whistle faded, replaced by the gentle clop of hooves. It being a Saturday, Price turned from the window and headed for McCullough's Livery on Main Street.

"Morning, Mr. McCullough," he said, his voice quiet among the men who spoke the subtle language of horses.

McCullough, a man with hands as tough as old leather, grunted from behind a copy of *The Greenville News*. "Morning, son. Awful news from up north." He tapped the headline with a thick finger.

EMPRESS OF IRELAND SINKS IN FOG; OVER A THOUSAND LIVES LOST

He shook his head. "Collided with a Norwegian coal ship in the St. Lawrence River. Gone in minutes."

Price nodded. The tragedy was immense—a horrifying thought—but in his world, it was a distant rumble, like thunder on the far side of the Blue Ridge Mountains.

His world was here: the ache of his father's absence, the quiet strength of his mother, and the familiar warmth of a horse's flank under his hand.

He ran a palm down the neck of a placid Walker-type

gaited mare, her calm temperament a hallmark of the Tennessee breed that prized smoothness over speed. She flicked her ears at the crinkle of a peppermint wrapper in his pocket.

"Your father," Mr. McCullough said, folding the paper with a sigh, "he didn't know the first thing about horses. But he knew people. Said he learned more about people in a stable than he ever did in a seminary."

A familiar pang of grief tightened in his chest—a hollow space the scent of pipe tobacco could no longer fill. He focused on the mare's soft eyes, a temporary anchor.

The news was just a headline. For now, the only lines that mattered were the reins in his hands and the invisible ties that bound him to the man he so dearly missed.

In the late afternoon, under a clouded sky, Price found himself drawn to the banks of the Reedy River. He needed to escape the apartment, where every object seemed to hold a ghost of his father.

He walked past the thunderous weave rooms of the mills, following the curve of the water until the roar of industry faded, replaced by the river's current and timeless murmur. He stopped at a familiar spot, a flat granite rock that jutted out over a deep, slow-moving pool.

This was their place.

It was here his father had taught him to cast a line, not with a fancy fly rod, but with a simple cane pole. The memory was so vivid it was painful. He could almost feel the warm weight of his father's hand on his shoulder, hear his voice, a low, patient rumble. '*Feel the line, feel the rhythm of the water,*' his father had said once, tapping a finger to his temple. '*The river has a map, Price. Most folks only see the surface.*' Then he'd tapped his chest. '*But the real map... the one that shows you the currents no one else can see... that one's in here.*' He uncorked an empty medicine bottle from his pocket, scratched a tiny cross on the glass with his penknife, and set it on the current. "*Maps are no good if you don't test them,*" his father said. "*Let's see where the river says this belongs.*"

Price picked up a flat stone, his fingers closing around its smooth surface. He wasn't a boy anymore. He was the man of the house, a title that felt borrowed, too large for his shoulders. He was supposed to be strong for his mother, to be the rock she could lean on. But here, as he stood beside the ghost of his larger-than-life father, the facade crumbled.

Grief was not a gentle sorrow; it was a physical thing, an ache in his chest that made it hard to breathe. It was the empty chair at the dinner table. It was the silence where a booming laugh should be. He thought of all the things left unsaid, the questions he'd never get to ask, the shared future that had been stolen from them in a single, silent heartbeat.

He drew his arm back and skipped the stone across the water's surface. One, two, three times it bounced, a fleeting moment of grace before it sank without a trace.

As the last ripple vanished, leaving the water's surface as smooth and indifferent as the sky, he made a promise. He could not bring his father back, but he could honor his memory. He could carry his father's strength, his unwavering decency. He could be the man his father had always believed he would become.

He stood a moment longer, the river's cool air a balm on his raw emotions, then turned and walked back toward the city. The promise he made was heavy in his gut, but it was also a direction.

Now, he just had to take the first step, though he had no idea where it would lead.

2

THE LEDGER - PART I
EVENING

The kerosene lamp on the kitchen table cast a warm circle of light, pushing back the evening gloom. The rest of the apartment was silent, save for the soft rhythm of Price's breathing from the other room.

For Sarah Hays, these late hours were her sanctuary, the only time she was not a teacher, a pastor's widow, or a mother, but simply herself.

Her husband had left behind a legacy of Presbyterian faith and service, but little in the way of financial security.

Sarah shouldered the burden without complaint.

During the school year, she taught at a small private academy for girls, her days filled with the patient instruction of children, her evenings with mending, baking, and ensuring that Price never felt the full weight of their lean circumstances.

Before her lay a compact, cloth-bound ledger, its pages were a testament to her resilience, filled with neat columns of figures written in a precise, elegant hand. On one side: income. Her modest salary from the girls' academy, and below it, "Price - $1.25," the meager but vital sum he contributed from the Livery.

On the other side was the relentless list of expenses: rent, flour, kerosene, and thread for mending. Each month was a delicate balancing act, a tightrope walk over a chasm of debt.

Her thoughts drifted to that afternoon. Mrs. Graham, wife of a church deacon, had pressed a basket into her hands —a loaf of bread, potatoes, a jar of jam. "Just a little something from the Ladies' Aid, dear," she had murmured, her voice loud enough for others on the street to hear.

Sarah accepted with a gracious smile, though her private pride stung at the public display. They only saw a pastor's widow, someone to be helped, a duty of public charity to be attended to.

In her ledger's neat columns, she was the architect of their survival. She looked at the ledger again, her finger tracing the entry for Price's earnings. She saw him growing into a man too quickly, his shoulders already learning to carry burdens that did not belong to him.

The coming summer on Sullivan's Island was a financial necessity, the wages from the Middletons a dam that would hold back the flood for another year.

With a soft sigh, she dipped her pen in the inkwell and made the final entry for the week. The numbers were close, closer than she liked, but they balanced.

She closed the ledger. She was not a victim. She was a mother, and her love for her son was an asset more valuable than any number in a book.

It was the only currency that would never run out.

3

THE CROSSING

JUNE 1914

The Lowcountry

The air on the platform was scented with coal smoke and steam from the waiting locomotive. Price and his mother, with their modest trunk and wicker baskets, stood and waited for their train as an island in the river of merchants and travelers.

The train ride was a four-hour trip from the rolling hills of the Upstate to the flat lands of the Lowcountry. Price sat glued to the window, watching the landscape change. The familiar pine forests of Greenville gradually gave way to cotton fields, then to dense swamps with trees draped in Spanish moss.

The air filtering through the open window grew heavier, thicker, and carried the briny scent of the sea. It was a smell that signaled a profound shift, not just in geography, but in the rhythm of his life.

In Charleston, they navigated the chaotic energy of the city to reach the ferry terminal. The ferry to Mount Pleasant was a noisy vessel, its deck crowded with laborers, soldiers, and returning summer families.

A hemp line and a tin sign stamped "COLORED" split the benches at the stern, where the air was thick with soot from the engine stack. Price noticed the sign and the line, the way people pretended not to see it.

A child laughed on the far side of the rope, her sound bright and unselfconscious, quickly swallowed by the engine's roar.

He thought of his father—the way he'd spoken from the pulpit against it, calling it not just man's law but a fundamental moral wrong. The words had cost him parishioners, but he'd never softened them.

Price looked back toward the sign and felt an uneasy mix of pride and shame—pride in the man his father was, shame at how little the world seemed to have listened.

In Mount Pleasant, they boarded the new trolley—the final leg of their pilgrimage—a marvel that had replaced the slow, sad trot of the mule-drawn cars only a few years earlier. Price watched as sparks snapped from the overhead wire.

The trolley was the island's lifeline. From the first stop in Mount Pleasant's old village, the car rattled down Pitt Street, past cottages and shops, before climbing onto the long wooden trestle bridge that spanned the cove.

From high atop the bridge, the blue-green salt marsh unfolded out the window—a sprawling expanse of sweetgrass dotted with the lonely figures of oystermen. Great snowy egrets stood like statues in the shallows, and the sharp, chattering cry of a hidden marsh bird echoed from the reeds, a wild sound untouched by the modern world rattling past.

The trolley rumbled over the water for what felt like an eternity before finally reaching Sullivan's Island, where it found its tracks on Middle Street.

For Price, this journey was more than just a trip; it was a shedding of his Greenville skin, a welcome return to a world of sun, salt, and the endless, rhythmic whisper of the ocean —the same rhythm his father had once called the ocean's true voice.

4

THE SHORE

JUNE 1914

Sullivan's Island

The Middletons' summer home was a sprawling, three-story affair of whitewashed siding and forest green shutters that sat on a low sand dune overlooking the ocean. Its wide, generous porches caught the cool sea breeze.

Sarah Hays found Mrs. Eleanor Middleton in the kitchen. She was sitting at a long wooden table, a large ceramic bowl in her lap, her fingers moving with a practiced rhythm as she shelled fresh peas. She looked up and smiled as Sarah entered.

"Sarah, there you are," she said, her voice warm and genuine. "Come, sit with me. This is a two-person job if we want them for dinner."

This was the way of things with the Middletons. There was no rigid line between employer and employee. Mrs. Middleton, a woman whose husband, Arthur, owned one of the most successful shipping lines in Charleston, never put on airs. She treated Sarah not as a servant, but as a trusted friend and confidante.

"How was the journey down?" Eleanor asked, pushing a smaller bowl toward Sarah.

"Smooth as it could be," Sarah replied, her hands falling into the familiar rhythm of shelling. "Price stared out the window the whole way. He loves the moment the air changes, when you can first smell the salt."

"He's a good boy, that one," Eleanor said thoughtfully. "You can see the strength in him. Arthur is always saying he wishes our William had a bit more of Price's grit. All William thinks about are his sailboat races." She sighed, a sound that was less about complaint and more about the universal worries of a mother.

"Arthur's business is expanding so quickly... new trade routes to the Caribbean. It's a blessing, of course, but it wears on him. Having you here, knowing the house is in your capable hands... it's a greater relief to him than you can imagine. You're the heart of this house in the summer, you know."

The compliment was delivered, without fanfare, and it settled in Sarah's heart like a warm stone. It was this unassuming dignity, this recognition of her worth beyond the wages she was paid, that made these summers bearable.

It was the reason she returned this year.

That afternoon, his mother shooed Price out of the cottage. "Go on," she said with a smile. "See if your old paths are still there." He walked barefoot toward the sound of the surf, his feet finding the familiar, packed-sand trails that wound through the dunes.

They were paths of convenience, shortcuts between the cottages and the sea, but they were almost invisible unless you knew where to look. Ghost paths, his father had once called them, trails meant for those who refused to follow the obvious road.

His path opened onto the vast expanse of the beach, and down the shore, he saw a lone figure. It was a girl in a simple white dress walking a dog near the water's edge. She was a splash of crisp, effortless grace against the wild backdrop of the sea, clearly from a different world.

Before he could even register the urge to walk closer, she turned and disappeared up a private path through the dunes, vanishing from sight.

5

MENDING

JUNE 1914

That evening, Price found his mother on the porch of their cottage, a mending basket in her lap. The sky was awash with the soft colors of the sunset, and the air was cooling. He sat on the top step, leaning his back against the post, the wood still warm from the day's sun.

"Tired?" she asked, her needle moving in a steady, even stitch.

"A little," he admitted. "Walked the whole length of the island, just about. It feels good to be back."

"Mrs. Middleton paid me the kindest compliment today," his mother said, her mending falling still. "She called me the heart of her home." A quiet pride filled her voice. "To be appreciated just for who you are, Price... that's a rare gift. Don't you ever forget it."

She looked at him, her expression soft in the fading light. "The Middletons are good people. They have wealth, yes, but they haven't let it poison their character. They understand that a person's worth isn't measured by the size of their house or their name in the society pages. It's measured by their integrity, by how they treat others."

She set her mending aside and looked out toward the darkening ocean. "You're going to meet all sorts of people in this life, especially on this island. Some will only see your worn trousers and the dirt on your hands. They'll judge you before you've spoken a word. Last year was different, you were protected by Mr. Middleton—he gave you work and a stipend to mow the lawn, paint, and do odd jobs. This year you are a young man heading out into the world."

The words were a mother's attempt to armor her son against the world's casual cruelties.

"The important thing," she continued, her voice a solid anchor in the twilight, "is that you never let them decide who you are. You know your worth. It's in here." She tapped her chest lightly. "Hold onto that."

Price didn't answer. He just watched the last sliver of sun disappear below the horizon, his mother's words settling over him, a contentment that felt as constant as the tide.

6

THE LEDGER - PART II

SUMMER 1914

W hat visitors didn't understand about the Lowcountry was that the mornings were cooler, but the humidity was at its thickest, making it seem the hottest part of the day. And Price's days began long before the sun had a chance to burn off the morning mist.

Every dollar he earned was a number in his mother's ledger, a little victory against the tide of their lean circumstances. This knowledge was a weight on his shoulders, but also a fuel.

Mr. Middleton had secured him a job as a civilian laborer at Fort Moultrie, the U.S. Army base and the economic hub of the island. Price was an apprentice on a masonry crew working on the newest fortifications, reinforced-concrete structures like Battery Gadsden and Battery Thomson, designed to house the latest in artillery.

Under the scorching sun, he and other laborers hauled timber, mixed oceans of concrete, and felt the day's wages being baked into their very bones. The heat was a physical enemy, reflecting off the sand and concrete, and sapping their strength. The air was thick with cement dust that coated their tongues and stung their eyes.

The old guns were gone. In their place stood "disappearing carriages"—clever mechanical mounts that used the force of the gun's recoil to rise to fire and then immediately sink back down, protecting the gun and its crew behind thick concrete parapets while they reloaded.

During a maintenance run at Battery Gadsden, a cable snapped—a crack like a rifle. The counterweight lurched and started down, dragging its line. A young laborer froze.

Price's McCullough's Livery instincts kicked in. He pointed to a chain fall hanging from a girder. "Snatch-block on that—now!" he barked, already grabbing the dangling tagline and flipping it over the sheave. "Haul!"

Three men hit the hand chain. The line bit. The counterweight slewed off its path and slammed to the floor, stopping inches from the boy's boots. The hoist shuddered to a stop. A wisp of smoke curled from the brake, and the top hook showed a thumb's-width of spread.

Later, the foreman pulled Price aside. "That was quick thinking, son," he said, out of earshot of the others. Then his voice hardened. "It was also a breach of protocol. You're not authorized to direct a crew."

He pressed Price's weekly pay into his hand, short by a dollar. "For the cost of the chain fall you damaged. We're even. Don't do it again." The injustice stung, a sharp reminder that doing the right thing sometimes came at a cost.

As he walked toward the stables to begin his second job, the day's weight pressed down on him. The near-disaster, the rebuke, the lost dollar—it all amounted to a deficit in his mother's ledger he couldn't explain. He was falling behind in a race he hadn't known he was running.

Price's second job was the ice route. The huge 300-pound ice blocks were brought over from the mainland by ferry, insulated under thick canvas tarps and sawdust. The wagon horse was a massive Percheron, a creature of pure, steady power whose breed was prized for pulling artillery, now reduced to the mundane task of hauling ice.

The giant steamed in the Lowcountry heat. He felt a pang for the magnificent animal, its powerful muscles slick with sweat under the brutal sun. Bred for battlefields or farm fields, it seemed a waste, a quiet tragedy, to see such nobility reduced to hauling ice in the sweltering heat.

Its driver, a man named Sal, grumbled as he secured the load. "Smell that?" he asked Price, gesturing with his chin toward the ice. "Ammonia residue. That's what they use to make this so-called 'Crystal Ice.' They call it progress. I preferred the old blocks cut from the frozen lakes up north."

His ice route took him along I'On Avenue, past the stately homes of Senior Officers' Row. He had learned to read the street like a map of rank: the lieutenants' quarters had two windows across the front, the captains' had three and a porch, and the commander's was a white fortress of absolute command at the end of the line.

His job was to deliver the ice to the wealthy homes, using weighty iron tongs to hoist smaller, fifty-pound blocks onto a burlap sling on his shoulder.

He was the invisible boy who came to the servant's back door, leaving a trail of meltwater on the kitchen steps, his presence acknowledged only by the clink of a few coins.

That evening, his muscles aching, Price made his final ice delivery to a large home on I'On Avenue. The servant, a young woman distracted by a pot boiling over, pressed the coins into his hand without looking.

As he walked back toward his cart, he counted them. She'd given him a quarter too much—a significant overpayment. For a fleeting, shameful moment, Price saw it not as a mistake, but as a correction. A way to reclaim what was unfairly taken.

The quarter was heavy in his palm. He thought of what it could buy. Then, he felt his father's gaze. He turned, walked back to the kitchen door, and handed the quarter back to the surprised servant. "You gave me too much," he said, and left before she could thank him.

From the back of the houses, he could hear the faint sounds of life from the front porches—polite laughter, the clinking of glasses filled with sweet tea or the newly fashionable Coca-Cola.

With each passing year, the contrast between his world and theirs seemed to widen. The officers' houses now blazed under the unwavering glare of electric porch lights, a marvel powered by the island's power plant.

That light cast sharp, clean shadows, a world without ambiguity. It stood in contrast to the dim, flickering kerosene lamp in his cottage, whose soft glow blurred the edges of their poverty but never hid it.

He knew which world he lived in. The world of the kerosene lamp. And he now feared it was a world from which there was no escape.

THE GIRL ON THE PORCH
SUMMER 1914

I t was from the shadow of one of the gnarled live oaks, its ancient branches draped in drifts of Spanish moss, that he first truly saw her.

She was on Colonel Chamberlain's porch, the base commanding officer's residence, a book resting in her lap.

Her gaze was fixed on the horizon, a restless energy in her posture. Being the Colonel's daughter, she was a princess in this island kingdom, yet there was a spark of defiance in her eyes.

She must have felt his gaze, for her head turned, and her eyes met his across the lawn as he carried the block of ice towards the back entrance.

There was no surprise in her look, only an unnerving curiosity. In her eyes, he didn't see the judgment he expected, but a flicker of recognition, as if she were seeing not the hired boy, but the man.

A call from inside the house broke the moment, and she disappeared.

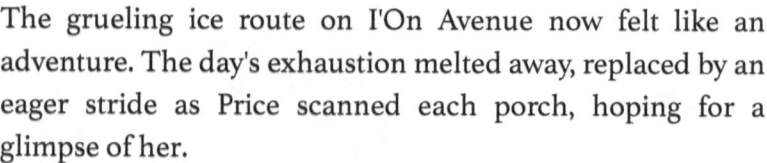

The grueling ice route on I'On Avenue now felt like an adventure. The day's exhaustion melted away, replaced by an eager stride as Price scanned each porch, hoping for a glimpse of her.

One afternoon, while delivering ice to the back of the house, Price heard voices from the side porch.

"Another set, Clara?" The man's voice was confident, laced with a playful challenge. "I believe the score is in my favor."

"Only because you distract me with your terrible stories, Lieutenant," Clara's voice replied, a light, musical laugh following. Price could picture the scene perfectly: the white wicker chairs, the tall glasses of sweet tea, the tennis rackets resting against the railing.

He lingered for a moment, hidden by the thick leaves of a magnolia tree. He saw the man lean forward, his expression earnest. "My father was speaking with General Wood just last week. There's talk of a post in the Philippines. It would be a fine advancement. A fine place to start a family."

The implication was as clear and bright as the afternoon sun. He wasn't just a suitor; he was the heir apparent.

A familiar, dull ache of otherness settled over him. This wasn't just a man; he was a representative of the world Price could never touch, a world that was already laying its claim on the girl on the porch.

But he had learned her name—Clara—Clara Chamberlain—a name he would never forget.

STORM WARRIORS - PART I

SUMMER 1914

O n an island divided by rank and wealth, Price found his only real companionship not on the manicured lawns of Officers' Row but on the wild shoreline. There he met Silas McGuire, a Surfman with the U.S. Life-Saving Service—a post that commanded respect across the island.

The Service was a rugged brotherhood of just six men and a keeper, their station a lonely outpost on the South Carolina coast. They were known as "storm warriors."

Price's friendship with Silas was forged not in conversation, but in shared labor. One evening, walking along the beach, Price saw Silas near the water's edge. The surfman was alone, his muscles corded with effort as he struggled with one of the station's massive surfboats.

The boat, a beast of white cedar and oak weighing nearly a thousand pounds, was half-on, half-off its wheeled launching carriage.

Price had seen the whole crew of six men handle the

boat with long, twelve-foot oars and knew this was no job for one man. He jogged up the beach toward him.

"Need a hand?" Price called out as he got closer.

Silas grunted, a flicker of surprise and relief in his eyes. "You got the back for it, kid?"

Price just squared his shoulders. Together, using a long timber as a lever, they managed to winch the last few feet of the heavy hull onto its cradle with a final, groaning thud.

The first battle was won, but the war was beginning. The boathouse stood a hundred yards away, and the path was soft, deep sand.

"All right," Silas panted, "now the fun part."

For the next twenty minutes, they strained in unison, their bare feet sinking, fighting for grip as they dragged the carriage through the sand. The wheels dug in, resisting every pull.

It was a grueling, torturous journey that left their muscles screaming and their lungs burning. When they finally got the carriage onto the wooden ramp and rolled it into the boathouse, Silas slumped against the boat's hull, breathing heavily.

"Appreciate that," Silas said, wiping a forearm across his sweaty brow. "More than you know." He gestured to the sprawling white building behind them. "This old boathouse has protected our boats through her share of storms, but she's never seen a boat put away by just two men."

"Why were you hauling it by yourself?" Price asked, confused. "Seems like a job for the whole crew."

A wry, self-deprecating grin touched Silas's lips. "Lost a bet," he admitted. "With the keeper, Captain Adams. I made the mistake of challenging him to a cook-off. I swear, that man's shrimp recipe is just salt and paprika. It's awful."

He shook his head with a chuckle. "Turns out the boys prefer the Captain's recipe. Loser gets boat-hauling duty alone for the week. Never trust the palate of men who chew tobacco all day, my friend."

The next evening, Price returned to the station just as Silas was beginning the solitary ritual again. He didn't say a word, just fell into step beside him.

He came back the next day, and the day after that.

For the rest of the week, they worked in companionable silence, the shared, brutal task forging a bond deeper than words could express.

By the end of the week, Silas just clapped him on the shoulder. "All right, kid. You got salt," he said, with respect in his gaze.

With his "punishment" served, Silas began showing Price the tools of their dangerous trade. He gestured to the Lyle Gun, a small cannon used to fire a shot line to a wrecked ship. His hand hesitated.

"Two winters ago," Silas said, his voice dropping, "a shrimper out of McClellanville got caught in a squall. The kid on duty hadn't properly faked the line in the box. When we fired, the line snarled. Snapped."

He ran his hand over a stiff, cork-block life vest. "We got there too late. Pulled three men from the water. Frozen. The fourth... we never found him."

"Everything has to be perfect," Silas said, his voice now a

low, hard whisper. "Out there, you don't get a second chance."

He gestured to the surfboat. "We're a brotherhood. The older men, they teach the younger ones the channels, the hidden sandbars, how to read the water. When every other sane captain is trying to get into a safe harbor, we have to go out. Each man leaves a wake for the next to follow. The service has a motto, you know." He paused, his eyes fixed on the horizon. "'You have to go out, but you don't have to come back.'"

Price looked puzzled. "I don't understand."

Silas's gaze hardened slightly, the levity gone, replaced by the grim reality of his calling. "It means be prepared for what's coming. Get your lines squared away—because when the call comes, you head into the storm and perform the rescue. But if you're not prepared—you won't make it back."

The words settled between them, a simple testament to the brutal reality of the life Silas had chosen.

"It's not a warning, Price. It's a promise we make to others. A good friend of mine—a young surfman named Coste, one of the best I ever knew—had just married the sweetest girl you ever saw when he drowned off Station 12, trying to save a woman and her boy caught in the rip. He was my responsibility. Captain Adams put him under my training. But Coste... he was young, strong, thought he could muscle his way through anything. He underestimated the storm. I told him, I showed him, but he never truly respected the power out there. He saw a family in trouble and charged straight in, right into the worst of it. Fought it until he had nothing left. I should have seen it in him—should've broken him of that pride before it got him killed. It's a heavy thing, having a man's life on your conscience. I'll be damned if I add another."

9

THE RIP - PART I

SUMMER 1914

A few days later, Price found Silas at the water's edge. Price watched as Silas pulled a glass bottle from a burlap sack, put an old piece of paper in it, sealed it with a cork, and tossed it into the churning foam.

"Sending out an SOS?" Price asked, a half-smile on his face.

Silas chuckled without turning. "Nah. Checking the rip." He tossed another bottle into the surf a few yards away. "Class is in session. Watch." Price watched, with a faded memory of his father throwing the medicine bottle in the Reedy River.

The first bottle bobbed aimlessly for a moment, then was slowly washed back toward the shore. But the second bottle, a few yards south, was caught by something unseen. It moved with unnatural speed, a straight, determined line heading directly out to sea, cutting against the direction of the incoming waves. It was a frightening display of the water's hidden power.

"See that?" Silas pointed. "That's the rip current. A river

in the ocean, flowing the wrong way. Most folks, they get caught in that, they panic. They try to swim straight back to shore, right against the current."

The bottle continued its rapid journey outward, a speck in the vast, gray ocean. It traveled fifty, then seventy-five, then more than one hundred yards before its progress slowed, and it began to drift lazily in the calmer water beyond the breakers.

"That's the kill zone." Silas said, his voice turning serious. "A man can be swept out four hundred feet from shore in the blink of an eye. From here to where that bottle stopped. You try to fight it and swim back in before you're past that point, you'll just wear yourself out. You'll tire, you'll drown. The ocean always wins that fight."

"So what do you do?" Price asked, his eyes still fixed on the distant bottle.

"You don't fight," Silas said.

"You let it take you. You just float, ride it out until you stop going out, just like that bottle did. Then, once the pull stops, you swim parallel to the shore. Get yourself out of the river. You swim fifty yards that way," he gestured down the beach, "and then you try to swim in. If you still feel the current, you swim further parallel, and then you try again. You don't fight the ocean's strength; you use your head to get out of its way."

10

THE UNDERTOW

SUMMER 1914

A s the last bottle drifted from view, Price and Silas sat on a dune, watching the retreating tide expose wet sand that mirrored the deep blue sky.

The stiff blades of seagrass whispered around them.

"You're a quiet kid," Silas observed, breaking the comfortable silence. He wasn't looking at Price, but at the sea. "Got a lot turning around in that head of yours."

Price shrugged, tracing a pattern in the sand with his finger. "Not much to say, I guess."

"Everyone's got something to say," Silas countered. "Where you from, really? Upstate, I hear."

"Greenville," Price answered. "My father was the pastor at the Presbyterian church there. Before he passed."

The admission hung in the air for a moment. Silas nodded slowly, a silent acknowledgment of a shared human experience. "My old man was a fisherman out of Murrells Inlet. Drowned in a squall when I was seventeen. The ocean gives, and the ocean takes."

He picked a blade of seagrass, put it between his teeth, and began to chew on it.

"Sometimes," Silas continued, his voice softer now, "the things that pull at you the hardest aren't in the water. They're right here." He tapped his chest.

"When my old man's boat went down... for two years, I was dead inside. Drank too much. Fought anyone who looked at me wrong. I was trying to swim back into a storm that had already passed. It nearly killed me."

He looked at Price then, his gaze direct, the wisdom in it now edged with the shadow of memory. "Same trick with grief," he said, his voice softer now. "You don't fight the pull. Ride it. When it eases, angle for shore."

Price looked at the ocean. For the first time, he had the unnerving and welcome sensation that someone saw the currents pulling at his heart.

In the presence of this "storm warrior," he felt a little less adrift.

11

THE BREAKERS

SUMMER 1914

With his shift finally over, Price stripped off his sweat-soaked work shirt and raced into the surf, the cool water a welcome relief. He dove through a breaking wave, washing away the day's grime.

He was making his way back to the shore, the water swirling around his waist, when he saw her.

She was walking near the water's edge, a small, energetic fox terrier straining at the end of a leather leash. It was Clara, the Colonel's daughter. She wore a simple pale yellow dress, its hem dancing in the sea breeze.

He had only ever seen her from a distance, a figure on a porch, a name whispered among the laborers. Up close, she had a presence that seemed to command the very shoreline.

As she drew nearer, the dog, spotting him, let out a series of sharp, excited yaps and began pulling her in his direction. A smile touched her lips as she expertly reined the animal in.

A sudden, acute awareness of his state sent a flush of heat up his neck—bare-chested, his work trousers soaked and clinging to his legs, his hair slicked back with saltwater. He stopped, intending to give her a wide berth.

But she walked straight toward him. Her gaze curious and unnervingly direct.

"He seems to have found a friend," she said as she reached him, her voice as clear and bright as the light on the water. The dog was now sitting at her feet, tail wagging, looking up at Price expectantly.

"He's a fine-looking dog," Price managed to say, the words feeling clumsy.

"He's a terror, is what he is," she laughed, a sound that seemed to catch the rhythm of the waves. "He digs up my mother's hydrangeas and chases squirrels with a ferocity that is frankly unbecoming."

Her eyes, a shade of blue that seemed to hold the depth of the ocean itself, met his. There was no judgment in them, only an open, intelligent curiosity. "You deliver ice, don't you?"

"Yes, ma'am," he said.

"Please don't call me ma'am. It makes me feel ancient. My name is Clara."

"Price Hays, at your service," he replied.

For a moment, they just stood there, kicking the surf washing over their ankles, caught in a silent, charged space where the island's rigid rules seemed to dissolve. He saw not the Colonel's daughter, but a flicker of the same restless spirit he felt in his soul.

And in his bare-shouldered strength and dignity, she saw something far more compelling than the polished officers who populated her father's porch.

This boy was different—he seemed to have a strength that came from the earth itself.

12

A SIGNAL

SUMMER 1914

A few days later, the air crisp after the humidity broke, Price made his rounds with a hopeful anticipation. Reaching the Chamberlain residence, he saw the signal—the ice card in the window. He hefted the fifty-pound block and made his way to the back of the house.

As he placed the block of ice into the top of the kitchen icebox, he felt her presence behind him, a warmth that had nothing to do with the temperature of the room.

Wiping his wet hands on his trousers, he turned to face her. "That should do it."

She held out her hand, not with the coins lying flat on her palm as the servants did, but with the coins held between her thumb and forefinger. As Price reached for them, her fingers deliberately brushed against his, a touch that was both fleeting and electric. It sent a jolt through him, a silent, unambiguous message.

"I walk Jasper at sunset," she said, her voice barely a whisper, her eyes holding his. "Near the old battery."

Then she was gone, the screen door closing with a soft click, leaving Price standing alone, the coins warm in his hand, his heart pounding a frantic rhythm against his ribs.

He raced through the rest of his route, his mind a blur. He hurried back to his cottage, scrubbing his hands and face with harsh lye soap until his skin was raw, trying to wash away the grime of his labor.

He put on his only other presentable shirt and trousers, the fabric worn but clean.

He met her where the Battery emplacements stood like sleeping giants against the darkening sky.

The path took them through a small patch of maritime woods, the air growing cooler and scented with pine as the last rays of sun slanted through the canopy of magnolia and cedar.

Jasper greeted him like an old friend before running off to chase the sandpipers. The sunset bled across the horizon in strokes of orange and fiery pink.

They walked, not touching, but the space between them was alive with unspoken words.

She told him of her life in Charleston, of a world of formal education and social obligation that felt like—an obligation. He laughed and told her of Greenville, of the mills, of his father, and of the abiding strength of his mother.

They were fascinated by the foreignness of each other's worlds, yet they recognized in each other a shared sense of being slightly out of place, of yearning for something more than the path laid out for them.

As darkness settled, wrapping the island in a blanket of

stars, he walked her to the edge of her lawn. The sounds of the crickets and the distant murmur of the ocean filled the silence.

"I have to go," she whispered, her face turned up to his in the faint moonlight. "If my father were to see us..."

The warning was clear. He was a secret, a thrilling and dangerous deviation from her life. He watched her slip away into the shadows of the manicured gardens, a ghost of white linen, before he turned and hurried away, the gravity of their stolen time a wonderful new burden on his heart.

13

CROSS TIDE

SUMMER 1914

T he next day, with a knot of hopeful anxiety in his stomach, Price saw the ice card in the Chamberlain's window and allowed himself a smile. He grabbed the heavy block, his mind replaying their conversation as he approached the back of the house.

He heard voices from the side lawn—he recognized Clara's laugh instantly, a light, bright sound that made his heart quicken. But then another voice joined hers, a man's, deeper and laced with a confident, easygoing familiarity.

"Your backhand has improved, Clara, but your serve is still far too charitable," the man's voice teased.

"And your sportsmanship is as dreadful as ever, Thomas Ordway Davies," Clara retorted, her tone playful.

Price stopped, frozen in place behind the hedge. He could hear the soft *thwack* of a tennis ball and the scuff of shoes on the grass court. Peeking through a gap in the leaves, he saw them.

They were both dressed in crisp whites, rackets in hand, their faces flushed from the game. Lieutenant Davies, a man

Price recognized from the fort, was handsome in the way of the officer class—tall, with a square jaw and an air of unshakeable self-assurance. He was leaning against the net, smiling at Clara in a way that was both proprietary and admiring.

Price felt a cold, familiar sensation wash over him. It wasn't the sharp sting of jealousy he might have expected. It was something heavier, a dull, resigned ache of otherness.

He saw Davies say something that made Clara laugh again, and he watched as the Lieutenant casually placed a hand on her arm. It was a gesture of casual ownership, a public and accepted intimacy.

Price set the ice on the back steps and left without a sound.

14

THE SPY GLASS

SUMMER 1914

He didn't see her for the rest of the week. The stern-faced servant was at the back door, or the coins for the ice were left on the counter, a silent dismissal. The hope that had bloomed in him after their sunset walk began to wither.

By the next night, a restless energy he couldn't contain drove him back to the beach. He told himself he was walking, just needed to feel the sand and sea, but his path led him inevitably toward the stretch of shore near the old battery.

And she was there.

She was walking Jasper, a solitary figure against the moonlit expanse of the ocean. She saw him approaching and stopped, a hopeful smile on her face.

"I was hoping you'd be here," she said, her voice soft. "I couldn't get away. My father has had... guests." The word was freighted with meaning. She meant Davies.

"I heard you," Price said, the words coming out before he could stop them. "Playing tennis."

A flicker of understanding, perhaps even guilt, crossed her face. "He is my father's choice," she said. It wasn't an apology, but a statement of fact, of the cage she was in. "He is not mine."

The simple declaration was enough. The space between them closed, and they walked in a comfortable silence, the dog running ahead.

She told him how Davies had been following her, how his presence felt like a constant surveillance. He suspected something, so she couldn't get away, but he said he had dinner plans in Charleston this evening, so she felt it was safe.

Unseen by either of them, from the shadowed balcony of a neighboring house, a figure watched.

Lieutenant Davies, a pair of military-issue field glasses raised to his eyes, observed the two figures in their own private world. Something sour rose in his throat. He lowered the glasses, the ache in his gut not just jealousy, but a bitter, familiar taste.

The image triggered a memory as sharp as a knife, transporting him instantly to a stable filled with the scent of hay and the soft glow of lantern light.

He saw the face of his Emily, a girl whose father was a groom, and heard her laugh—the only honest sound he had ever known. He remembered her embrace, her kiss, and the senator's letter that had followed on cream paper: *End it. Your career requires a wife of suitable station.*

He had obeyed, and could still taste the bitterness of that choice, the gutting shame of choosing the uniform over his own heart. The knot in his stomach hardened. He had sacrificed his heart to the rigid order of this world. He would not stand by and watch the ice boy, ignorant of the cost, defy the very rules that had broken him.

He turned from the balcony and made his way directly to Colonel Chamberlain's front door. The order he had so painfully submitted to must be upheld. He told himself it was a matter of duty.

15

THE COLONEL

SUMMER 1914

Secrets, on an island as small as Sullivan's, have a short lifespan. And Colonel Chamberlain's network was vast—he took it upon himself to know everything that was happening on what he saw as his island. He was not surprised when Lt. Davies confirmed that there was more to the lingering glances between his daughter and the handsome ice boy.

After one night's delivery, he had the head servant summon Price to the spartan office hidden away at the back of the house. The Colonel's voice was calm, but his judgment was as swift and absolute as a saber stroke.

"My daughter is fond of you, son," he began, his tone devoid of malice but firm with the certainty of his world. "Who are you? What stock do you come from?"

Price met his gaze, his own unwavering. "My father was the Reverend Hays, sir. Of the Greenville Presbyterian church."

The Colonel paused, taking in the information. The past tense of "was" did not escape him, nor did the fact that the boy came from a man of God, a learned man. Still, the order of his world had to be maintained.

"I can see you are a hardworking young man," he said finally. "But you must understand your position. And hers." He didn't need to say more.

The words hung in the air, a final, unassailable verdict. There was a natural order to things, his calm demeanor implied, a hierarchy as carefully constructed as the military ranks on his collar. Price was not part of that order. He was a summer fixture, as temporary as the tides.

The Colonel's judgment simply illuminated the wall of class and expectation that was as solid and immovable as the granite jetties holding back the sea.

After Price had gone, the screen door clicked softly shut behind him. From the back of the house, Colonel Chamberlain returned to his stately office in the front. He remained at his desk for a long time.

The afternoon heat was oppressive, but the air felt still for other reasons, too. He had done what duty demanded—both as an officer and as a father. He had reinforced the unbreachable wall between his world and that of the hired boy from upstate. It had been a clean, swift maneuver—no different than securing a flank.

Yet a disquiet settled over him. On the corner of his desk sat a framed photograph of a younger version of himself—a brand-new captain standing straight beside another young officer.

The friend's name was Major John Egan. He had died at San Juan Hill, charging up a slope military logic had deemed impossible. Egan had been a farmer's son from Ohio, a man with no family connections but a fire in his eyes that shamed the well-bred sons of generals.

The Colonel picked up the photograph, the worn silver frame cool against his thumb. He saw that same fire in the Hays boy's eyes. It wasn't defiance—not precisely. It was something else. An unyielding integrity. A refusal to be bowed by circumstance.

The boy had met his gaze without flinching, his shoulders squared not with arrogance, but with a bone-weary dignity. He had seen officers with half that resolve break in the field—pedigree melting to panic under fire.

Hays was a minister's son—son of a man of the cloth— left to haul ice. There was a dislocation in it, a waste of good stock that pricked at the Colonel's sense of order.

His thoughts drifted back to a simpler time, a sweltering night in a tent outside Tampa, the air thick with mosquitoes and the smell of canvas. He and Egan had been arguing over a recent West Point appointee, a senator's son with a notoriously weak character.

"Mark my words, Chamberlain," Egan had said, running a rag along the barrel of his revolver, his voice a low, passionate rumble. "This army's obsession with pedigree over performance will be the death of us. They promote the name, not the man. You give me one man with grit—be he a farmer's son or a millhand—over ten of those silver-spooned cadets who've never had to fight for a damned thing in their lives. The battlefield doesn't give a damn about your father's signature on a letterhead. It asks only one question: can you lead?"

The Colonel had spent a career since then enforcing the Army's rigid hierarchy—a system built on the very pedigree

Egan had railed against. He believed in it; it was the bedrock of a functioning military. But he had also seen that true courage—the kind that turned the tide of battle—often came from the most unlikely of places. It came from men like Egan. Men, perhaps, like Hays.

He had dismissed the boy as unworthy of his daughter, yet he could not shake the feeling that he had misjudged the true measure of the man.

His gaze drifted from the photograph of his fallen friend to the stack of papers on his desk—a list of candidates for the new scholarship slot at The Citadel. He studied the names, the ink glistening in the lamplight. For years, he had quoted Egan's lessons without ever living them.

"Egan would've seen this differently," he murmured—not as an excuse, but as permission.

Then he picked up his pen and added a new name—the straightest line he'd ever drawn between who a boy was and who he might become.

Hays, G. P.

As darkness fell across the Colonel's study, Clara knocked and was permitted entry. She stood before his desk, a brochure for Vassar College clutched in her hand.

"Father, I wish to apply," she said, her voice steady. "They have a noteworthy program in civics and economics—"

"A subject for men who intend to govern," Colonel Chamberlain interrupted, not unkindly. "Your education is complete, Clara. You are prepared to be the wife of an officer. That is an honorable and vital station."

"It is a supportive one," Clara countered, a spark of defiance flashing in her eyes. "I do not wish to merely support a career. I wish to have one. To understand the world as you do. To debate policy, not just seating arrangements."

The Colonel sighed. "This is a passing fancy, brought on by these new suffragette ideas. The matter is closed. Do you acknowledge?"

Clara stood for a moment, the brochure crinkling in her fist. Then she replied as she had been raised, "Yes, sir."

She felt the air in the grand study grow thin, the scent of her father's cigars and leather-bound books suddenly suffocating.

16

THE SECRET

SUMMER 1914

The Colonel's edict fell between them. Their relationship became a thing of stolen glances and fleeting moments. When he delivered ice to their kitchen, if anyone else was present, Clara kept her back to him. For Price, it was a constant reminder of his inadequacy, a scar he carried through his long, hot days.

For Clara, it was a different kind of confinement. Her father's watchfulness was relentless, and her days were now carefully curated by a schedule set by her mother's social engagements.

The dismissal of her Vassar ambitions was a sharp reminder of the limits of her world. First, her heart. Now, her education. Thwarted at every turn, she retreated into the only space that was truly her own: her bedroom.

Before taking out her stationery, she knelt and retrieved a book from its hiding place between the heavy mattresses of her bed. She didn't open it. She just held it, the sharp corners of Mrs. Wharton's novel, *The Custom of the Country*, a silent rebellion in the palm of her hand.

It felt like holding a journey to a world she was not yet brave enough to discover. It was in this state of quiet defiance that she finally reached for her pen.

Letter from Clara

My dearest Price,

I write this knowing you will never receive it. I have no safe place to send it, no confidante I can trust. But my heart aches with the weight of words unspoken.

They judge you unworthy because your clothes are worn, because you labor in the sun. They see the surface, and they are fools. I see what they cannot: a strength that has been forged, not inherited.

When I look at the officers on my father's porch, with their easy laughter and polished boots, I see men playing a part. When I look at you, I see a man who can carry the world on his shoulders. You, with your quiet dignity, are more real than any of them.

And that is why they are afraid of you.

And why I am so drawn to you.

Yours,

Clara

She folded the letter, the sharp creases a poor container for the passionate words within. For a moment, she considered her jewelry box, but dismissed the thought; her mother or sister, borrowing a brooch, might happen upon it.

Even her bedroom was not a space entirely hers. Instead, she knelt, lifting the heavy corner of her mattress. The space beneath was cool and silent. She slid the letter into the darkness, a confession not just to Price, but to the dust and shadows.

As she let the mattress fall with a soft thud, she felt the familiar ache of her silence. The letter was a fantasy she could indulge in, but her reality remained unchanged, locked away just as securely as the words she had just hidden.

17

THE FIRST FALL

SUMMER 1914

A week later, a late summons for a final ice delivery brought him to the Chamberlain residence. The party was a glittering spectacle, electric lights casting a magical glow over officers in crisp white uniforms and women in pastel gowns.

From the shadows of the garden, he watched Clara dancing with Lieutenant Davies. They moved with an effortless, practiced grace, a picture of perfect compatibility that was a dull ache in his chest. He turned away, heading for the kitchen.

The path to the back of the house was slick with moss and condensation from the humid night air. His foot slipped. For a heart-stopping second, he fought for balance, a clumsy, desperate dance against gravity. The weight of the ice was too much. He went down.

He went down hard.

The fifty-pound block crashed onto the stone patio at the base of the porch steps with a sound like a gunshot. It did not just break; it exploded, shattering into glittering shards.

The music from the bandstand screeched to a halt.

A waltz died mid-note. On the porches, officers instinctively rushed to the railings, their military training compelling them to race in defense to the sharp, gunshot-like crack.

In the sudden, ringing silence, Price was the center of a hundred accusing stares, a stain on their perfect, glowing world. Humiliation, hot and sharp, washed over him.

Lieutenant Davies, seeing his opportunity, detached himself from Clara and walked to the top of the porch steps, a look of theatrical disgust on his face. "Well, well," he said, his voice carrying down into the silent garden. "It seems the help is literally trying to crash our party. Hey, Ice Boy—go fetch a mop before this melts all over the patio stones and makes them slick."

A wave of muffled, polite laughter rippled through the guests—not a roar, but the condescending titter of a crowd enjoying an unexpected bit of drama at someone else's expense. Price, his knee throbbing, began to gather the largest pieces of ice, his face burning.

Then, a voice cut through the mockery. "It was an accident, Lieutenant." Clara descended the steps from the porch, her eyes flashing with a cold fire Price had never seen. "There is no need for cruelty."

In a shocking breach of etiquette, she knelt on the patio, her delicate silk gown brushing against the wet, gritty stones, and began to help him. Together, in a shared, silent act of defiance, they picked up the largest pieces of ice and carried them to the edge of the patio, placing them in the soft grass of a flower bed.

The crowd went silent again, this time in stunned disbelief.

Before Davies could respond, another voice, calm and full of absolute authority, spoke from the top of the porch.

"Lieutenant." Colonel Chamberlain had been watching the entire exchange, his eyes dark, like chips of coal. He wasn't looking at the shattered ice, but at Davies. "Your concern for the safety of my guests is noted. Your public display of cruelty is not. You will rejoin the party." He then turned his head slightly toward the bandstand, his voice carrying with effortless command. "Music."

It was a clear, cold dismissal of the man, not the problem. Davies's face flushed a deep crimson. He gave a stiff, formal bow before turning on his heel and retreating back into the heart of the party.

The Colonel's gaze then fell on Price and Clara, who had slowly gotten to their feet. For a long moment, he looked at them. The Colonel gave a single, almost imperceptible nod —not of approval, but of something more profound: respect for the way they had handled themselves.

Price, with Clara still at his side, gave her a look of gratitude, nodded once to the Colonel, and then walked away, leaving the glittering party behind.

He had been publicly humiliated, but as he disappeared into the darkness, he did not feel defeated. He had stood his ground, and he had not been alone.

18

THE DANCE

SUMMER 1914

He found his way on a path through the maritime forest to the boneyard, the skeletal trees offering a strange comfort. He sank onto a piece of weathered driftwood, his head in his hands. He didn't hear her approach until she was standing over him.

"I am so sorry, Price," Clara whispered.

"It's not your fault," he said, his voice flat. "He was right. I don't belong here."

"No," she said, her voice fierce.

She took his hand. "He was wrong. They are wrong. They live in a world of uniforms and rules. They can't see what I see."

She turned to face him. "You are strong, honorable—I can see it in you. Don't let them make you believe you are anything less."

Her faith was a balm to his spirit.

A week later, another gathering took place on the island, a moonlit fundraiser for the church. Price had no invitation and was walking home when the sound of the orchestra and the warm glow of paper lanterns from the Chamberlain's back garden drew him closer.

He kept to the service alley that ran behind the great houses, pausing in the shadows near the carriage house. The music was a muffled, gentle waltz on the still night air, and through the garden, he could catch glimpses of silhouettes moving on the grand back porch.

It was a fool's errand, this hopeful vigil, and he knew it. He was about to turn away when a figure detached itself from the glow of the party and walked to the porch railing. It was Clara.

She must have felt his gaze. She looked out into the darkness, her eyes searching the shadows, and she saw him. For a heart-stopping moment, the world narrowed to the space between them. The laughter and music from the porch faded to a distant hum; all he could see were her eyes finding his in the shadows.

It was a silent, dangerous acknowledgment across a social chasm. He saw her make a decision. With a word to her companions, she slipped away from the light. A moment later, she appeared at the end of the garden path, a pale silhouette of silk against the night.

"I hoped you'd be here," she whispered, her voice breathless as she reached him.

"I shouldn't be," he said, the words aching with the truth of his position, taking an involuntary step back into the shadows.

"Then be here with me," she insisted, closing the space between them. She took his hand, her fingers warm against his calloused skin, and led him past the silent bulk of the carriage house to a flagstone patio.

It was their hidden world, tucked away behind a thick wall of azalea bushes, the air touched by the sweet perfume of jasmine climbing the trellis. The orchestra music was faint here, a ghost of a melody.

"They're playing our song," she said with a soft smile, though they had never had one.

Without a word, he put one hand on her waist, the fabric of her dress impossibly delicate beneath his rough touch. She rested her other hand on his shoulder, and they began to move, a slow, hesitant dance in the semi-darkness.

This was a swaying, elemental rhythm, guided not by music but by the beat of their hearts. He could feel the warmth of her through the thin silk, smell the scent of gardenia in her hair. He looked down at her, her face upturned to his in the moonlight, her eyes shining with a defiant, brilliant light.

In that moment, she was not the Colonel's daughter, and he was not the hired boy. They were just two people, holding on to each other against a world determined to keep them apart.

The risk of being discovered was a palpable heat between them, making every stolen second, every soft breath, feel charged and vital. It was an intimacy of thrilling, beautiful rebellion.

19

THE TENTH STATION - PART I

SUMMER 1914

The storm arrived without warning, a malevolence of dark clouds sweeping from inland, covering the beach before racing out to sea. The pleasant afternoon collapsed into chaos as wind and rain lashed the island.

A group of swimmers was caught off guard. Most scrambled back to shore, but two women, friends visiting the Chamberlain family, were caught in a vicious rip current near the beach access known locally as the Tenth Station—named for the trolley stop that marked the spot, a name now etched into the island's geography.

"Look!" someone screamed over the wind. "They're being pulled out!" The roar of the wind and waves swallowed their cries for help. A woman's voice—shrill, breaking —and then the sound vanished beneath the surf's thunder. The sea had swallowed them.

The surfboat was out for drill, nearly a thousand yards offshore, the men pulling in steady rhythm when the squall struck. From the stern, Silas raised his brass spyglass and scanned the shoreline. Through the glass, he caught flashes of pale limbs in the surf—two women trapped in the rip.

"Hard for the women! Ten o'clock, starboard!" he shouted. The oars bit water as the crew came about. A knot of movement caught his eye near the Tenth. Even from this distance, something was wrong. Before the bow swung, he saw a runner break from the crowd. Price.

Silas froze, his hands gripping the gunwale as the surfboat pitched. The world narrowed to the lone figure running along the shore. His chest tightened—the memory of Coste, the woman, the child, and the sea that took them all. He watched, helpless and terrified, as he was about to witness the same tragedy again.

On the beach, Price sprinted down the sand, then turned parallel to the swimmers for fifty yards before plunging into the churning water well north of their position.

But the storm had changed the rip's geometry. It wasn't a simple river flowing out to sea; it was a swirling, unpredictable vortex. The rip had moved, and now he was caught in it. He stopped and treaded water, letting the river take him out, one hundred, two hundred, three hundred feet into the sea.

When the current finally stopped, he swam parallel to the shore, then, in a jolt of panic, he realized a secondary current grabbed him, weaker but still pulling him out another hundred feet. He was still in the rip.

He swallowed a mouthful of saltwater and choked, his lungs burning. He saw one of the women go under, her head bobbing back up, her cries weaker now. Silas's lesson was for a standard rip, not this chaos. It wasn't working.

Improvise. He remembered the way the water died and broke against the old granite jetties that lined the harbor entrance farther south. It was a longer, more exhausting journey for him, but the rocks could break the current's power.

"FORGET THE BEACH!" he screamed, his voice raw against the wind. "THE ROCKS! SWIM FOR THE ROCKS!"

He reached the first woman and grabbed her arm. "Don't fight it! Sideways! Angle for the jetty!" he yelled, pointing toward the dark shape of the rocks. Together, they fought their way toward the jetty, picking up the second woman along the way as she had drifted farther, the cross-currents battering them.

Finally, they reached the wave-battered jetty—bruised, bleeding, scraping their way over the barnacles to the top, utterly exhausted—but alive.

Farther out, the surfboat clawed its way toward the jetty, oars rising and falling in uneven rhythm. Silas stood in the bow, scanning the rocks through the rain. When he saw Price helping the women up, he let out a breath he hadn't known he was holding.

Exhausted, Price fell to his knees, breathing harder and heavier than he ever had before. As he caught his breath, he saw a crowd gathering on the jetty. Among them was Colonel Chamberlain.

The Colonel's face was unreadable, a mask of professional calm, but his eyes, sharp and assessing, followed Price's every move. He watched as Price helped the trembling women to their feet, his exhaustion forgotten.

Dozens had witnessed the rescue. In that moment, Price was no longer the hired boy; he was something else—something the island hadn't yet figured out what to do with.

The Colonel approached, his boots making a heavy sound on the granite. He didn't offer praise. He looked at Price, then at the two shaken women. "Report, son," he said, his voice the calm, authoritative tone of a commander assessing a battlefield. "What happened out there?"

Price, still catching his breath, gave a clipped, factual account of the rip current. The Colonel listened without interruption, his gaze never leaving Price's face.

When Price finished, the Colonel gave a single, almost imperceptible nod. "Well done," he said, the words clipped and formal.

He then turned his attention to the rescued women, his duty shifting to the civilians now under his purview.

The next morning, the surf still heaved under a gray sky. Silas found Price by the boathouse, hauling wet rope into neat coils. For a long moment, neither spoke.

"You kept your head out there," Silas said finally. "Didn't fight it. Coste would've been proud."

Price looked up, eyes rimmed red from salt and exhaustion. "You taught me not to fight the water," he said. "To read it."

Silas gave a slow nod, his weathered face unreadable. "Aye. But reading it and living through it are two different things."

The wind carried the scent of the sea between them— respect, unspoken but understood.

A few days later, a summons arrived. It was not a casual note, but a formal invitation delivered by an orderly. The Colonel was not inviting him for a chat; he was commanding his presence for dinner.

20

THE STUDY

SUMMER 1914

Price spent the next forty-eight hours in a state of managed panic. His mother hemmed and took in a pair of his father's old linen trousers and pressed his one good shirt with an iron heated on the coal stove.

When he presented himself at the Chamberlains' front door, heart hammering against his ribs, he felt like a spy infiltrating enemy territory. The house, which he had only ever glimpsed from the outside or its service entrance, was a revelation.

A grand staircase of polished mahogany swept upward into the shadows of the second floor. The air inside was cool, stirred by an electric fan that whirred from a stand in the hall, and smelled of lemon oil and the sweet scent of roses. This was not just a home; it was a declaration of order and affluence.

Clara met him in the foyer, her smile a beacon. "Price, I'm so glad you could come." She introduced him to her family in the parlor, a room of high ceilings and thick silk curtains.

Colonel Chamberlain was imposing even out of uniform, and Mrs. Chamberlain, a woman with kind but appraising eyes, offered a polite, measured welcome.

Clara's older sister, Eleanor, was there with her fiancé, Henry Gable, a Charleston shipping merchant whose suit was impeccably tailored. Price shook their hands, aware of his meager outfit.

Dinner was an exercise in polite terror. Price found himself navigating a minefield of unfamiliar silverware. The table was an expanse of white linen, set with delicate porcelain and crystal that seemed to chime with every nervous movement.

A uniformed maid served the meal in silent, efficient courses: a creamy she-crab soup, followed by poached flounder with shrimp hollandaise, steamed asparagus, and sesame-seed wafers. Price watched, choosing the right fork by imitation.

The conversation, steered by the Colonel, soon turned to the war in Europe. The German invasion of Belgium dominated the headlines. "It's a European affair," Henry Gable stated. "Tragic, but think what our involvement would do to commerce. The British blockade is already playing havoc with my shipping schedules."

"Commerce is a poor reason to ignore tyranny, Henry," the Colonel countered, his voice calm but firm. "The Germans' violation of Belgian neutrality is a troubling precedent. An army that doesn't respect borders is a threat to all borders. Still, President Wilson is right to counsel neutrality. We are not prepared for a war of that scale."

Eleanor shivered delicately. "The papers are filled with such awful stories. It's all I can think about." Mrs. Chamberlain turned her kind eyes to Price. "And what are your thoughts, Mr. Hays? You've been very quiet."

Caught off guard, Price swallowed. "I don't know much about strategy, ma'am," he said honestly. "But my father, he was a Presbyterian minister, he used to say that you can judge a man's character by how he treats those with less power. It seems the same might be true of nations."

A thoughtful silence fell over the table. Price felt his face flush, certain he had overstepped. But then Colonel Chamberlain gave a single, approving nod. He looked down the table at Price, his expression confirming a judgment he had already made. "Spoken like a true pastor's son," he murmured, a note of deep respect in his voice. "Well said."

After dinner, Clara stood. "Mother, I was hoping to show Price the new electric lamp in Father's study. He's never seen one up close." "A fine idea, dear," Mrs. Chamberlain said with a smile. Clara's subterfuge worked perfectly.

Clara led Price down a long hall to the Colonel's study, a sanctuary of leather-bound books and the scent of cigars. On the massive oak desk sat a brass lamp with a green glass shade. "This is Father's pride," she whispered. "An Edison bulb."

Price reached out, his fingers hesitating over the small turn-key. He gave it a twist. A soft click, and the room was flooded with a bright, clean light—no hiss, no smoke, no smell of kerosene. He turned it off, plunging them into darkness, then on again, fascinated by the instant, magical transformation. The simple act was a marvel.

"It's amazing," he breathed.

"Leave it off," Clara whispered from the darkness. He felt her move closer, the rustle of her dress a soft sound in the stillness. She took his hand and led him away from the desk, into the shadows near the tall window. And there, in the dark, she turned to face him and put her arms around his neck.

He pulled her to him, and their lips met in a kiss that was both hesitant and hungry. In that embrace, his hands tracing the lines of her back, he felt the impossible warmth of her press against him, the rustle of silk, her breath a soft catch against his cheek—a jolt of joy and love so powerful it left him breathless.

The soft click of the doorknob was the only warning they had. The door swung open, silhouetting a figure against the light from the hall. It was the Colonel.

Clara gasped and sprang back, her hand flying to her mouth. Price, his heart pounding, did not move. He stood his ground and faced the Colonel, his posture straight, his expression unreadable.

Colonel Chamberlain stepped into the room and closed the door, plunging them into near-total darkness. The only sound was the whirring of the fan from the hall. He walked calmly to his desk and twisted the key on the lamp. The study was suddenly flooded with an interrogator's light.

He looked from Price's steady gaze to his daughter's flustered expression. "Clara," he said, his voice a low, even command that brooked no argument. "Your mother is asking for you in the parlor."

Clara hesitated, her eyes darting between her father and Price. Then, with a muted "Yes, sir," she hurried from the room, leaving the two men alone in silence.

The Colonel gestured to the leather wingback chair. "Sit down, Mr. Hays."

Price sat. The Colonel remained standing, regarding him

for a long, appraising moment. He thought again of his old friend, Egan. He saw that same fire in this boy's eyes.

"I've been a soldier a long time, Hays," he began. "I recognize courage. But what you did out there... You assessed a tactical problem and solved it under extreme duress. You didn't just react; you read the danger and charted a new course. The Army needs men who can find a safe path through chaos for others to follow."

He paused, his eyes searching Price's. "I've made inquiries. I know your circumstances. An opportunity exists for a young man of caliber—a sponsorship to The Citadel. It would not be a gift. It would be a trial. Do you have any ambition beyond this island, Mr. Hays?"

The question landed. Price was stunned into silence. He hadn't dared to articulate his restless yearning, the feeling of being trapped between the world of the mills and a future he couldn't yet see. In the Colonel's eyes, he saw not judgment but something unexpected—a recognition that felt like light breaking through storm clouds.

"Sir," Price finally managed, his voice hoarse. "I want to be a man my father would have been proud of. I want to lead a life of purpose."

"I recognize your courage, Hays. But courage alone does not make an officer. The Citadel requires a foundation in academics. I've reviewed your records. Let me be clear. The entrance examination is designed to weed out boys exactly like you. It is academically brutal, with a heavy emphasis on mathematics and classical languages. Your mathematics is... adequate, at best. Your Latin is non-existent. A sponsorship from me only gets your application reviewed. You would still need to pass the entrance examination. On your own merits.

And you would need a character reference from a commissioned officer on this post."

Price's heart sank. Another test. And, a reference? The only officer he even vaguely knew was Lieutenant Davies.

The Colonel saw the look on his face. "Yes," he said, a flicker of a smile on his lips. "It is a trial. The Army needs men who can overcome obstacles, not just physical ones. Think on it."

21

THE CITADEL

SUMMER 1914

That evening, he found his mother on the small porch of their cottage, a mending basket in her lap. The offer from the Colonel hung in the air between them, a thing of immense hope and terrifying weight.

"The Citadel," she said, her needle pausing mid-stitch. "Your father would have been so proud." She looked up, her eyes searching his in the fading light.

"This is a great opportunity, Price. A door opening to a world we never could have dreamed of. But that world... it will try to change you. They will measure you by the cut of your uniform and the name of your family, not by the strength of your character."

She set her mending aside. "Your father's name was respected because he was a decent man. He treated the mill owner and the laborer with the same kindness. That is your inheritance, Price. I know the temptations in a world that has so much when we have so little. I saw the look on your face the other night when you came home from your route.

The exhaustion, but something else. A struggle. You carry a compass inside you that points toward decency. Do not let them break it. Hold onto it. Do not let them convince you that their compass is better than yours. Promise me."

"I promise, Mama," he said, his voice thick with an emotion he couldn't name. But as he looked toward the uncertain future, a flicker of doubt shadowed his resolve.

It was one thing to make a promise on a porch; it would be another thing entirely to keep it in a world designed to break men like him.

22

THE LIEUTENANT - PART I

SUMMER 1914

P rice's rescue at the Tenth Station had transformed him overnight. He was no longer the invisible ice boy; he was a local hero, his name spoken with respect on the very porches from which he'd once been ignored.

The shift was intoxicating, but it also painted a target on his back. For Lieutenant Davies, the public adoration for Price, especially from Clara, was a bitter defeat.

A few days later, Davies found Price and Silas fishing near the docks. It was obvious he was looking for them, looking for a fight. The Lieutenant was flanked by two large officers, and he approached them with a swagger. "Well, if it isn't the Upstate hero of the hour," Davies began, his voice condescending. "Quite the little swimmer, Hays. But can you handle yourself like a man on dry land?"

Silas slowly set down his fishing pole, his eyes calm and watchful as the tide, fixing on Davies. "He handles himself just fine, Lieutenant. Is there a problem?"

Davies ignored him, his focus entirely on Price. "A bit of

sport," he said, a cruel smile playing on his lips. "A horse race. Down Middle Street, from the fort to the lighthouse, Station 12 to Station 18. A simple contest to see who the better man is, once and for all. Unless, of course, the delivery boy is afraid of a little competition."

The challenge, delivered loudly for the benefit of the gathered onlookers, was a public gauntlet thrown down. To refuse would be to admit defeat, to validate every sneer Davies had ever directed his way.

Price wiped his hands on his trousers and stood slowly, his expression neutral. "I'll race you."

23

THE RACE

AUGUST 1914

The news of the race spread through the island like wildfire. It was more than a contest; it was a battle of class and pride.

Davies, leveraging his rank and connections, secured the finest mount at Fort Moultrie. Ares was everything his name implied—a Cleveland Bay bred for war. Massive in the chest, with a stride that rolled like a thunderclap, he fought the bit until foam flew from his lips. Every ounce of him was pure conquest.

Price, by contrast, had nothing. The humiliation was the point.

That evening, his mother, her face etched with determination, went to the main house. Unbeknownst to Price, she pleaded with Mr. Middleton, her voice thick with the pride of a mother. "My boy is a good boy," she said, her hands clasped. "He's honorable. He cannot be shamed like this."

Moved by her words and the story of Price's heroism, Arthur Middleton, a man whose integrity matched his wealth, agreed without hesitation. "He can ride Mercury," he declared. "My personal saddle horse."

Mercury was an American Saddlebred, a bay gelding of finer lines than the brute warhorse he was up against. He was a gentleman's horse, with the intelligent eyes of a horse built for partnership, not conquest. He was built for grace, not raw speed.

Price leaned low over the gelding's neck, feeling the heartbeat beneath. "It's not about power, boy," he whispered, stroking his withers. "It's about trust."

As Price led Mercury from the stables, a surge of gratitude warmed him, though it couldn't loosen the knot of dread in his stomach. On paper, it was no contest.

Silas met him as he walked the horse toward the cottage. He ran a practiced hand down Mercury's leg, his expression thoughtful. "He's a fine animal, Price. But he's not a sprinter. Ares will try to win it in the first hundred yards."

"I know," Price said, his voice tight with worry.

Silas looked from the horse to Price, a smile touching his lips. "Good. Because this isn't a race of speed. It's a race of strategy. Just like the rip current. You don't fight the ocean's power head-on. You use your head to get out of its way. Same thing here. Let Davies fight his horse. You just ride yours."

The day of the race, all of Sullivan's Island gathered along Middle Street. Officers and their wives stood on porches, their sympathies clearly with Davies. The year-round residents, the fishermen and laborers, stood in the dusty street, beneath the shade of salt-stunted live oaks and palmetto trees. Their hopes rested on the boy from the Upstate.

Clara was there, her expression a mixture of hope and

anxiety, a touch for herself and her stature, but mainly for the boy who was beginning to win her summer heart.

At Station 18 near the Charleston Light, which served as the finish line, Arthur and Eleanor Middleton stood with Sarah Hays and Silas.

As the starting pistol cracked in the distance, Sarah spun around, her face pale. "I can't watch, Eleanor," she whispered, turning her back to the street. "I just can't."

Arthur Middleton put a reassuring hand on her shoulder. "It's all right, Sarah, I'll be your eyes," he said, his voice calm but charged with excitement.

"They're off!"

When the pistol cracked, Ares lunged forward in fury, but Mercury waited a heartbeat, then surged smooth and balanced, as though horse and rider shared one breath.

Arthur, using field glasses, announced for all to hear, "Davies on that brute Ares has taken a powerful lead... He's pulling away, a full two lengths ahead... Price is holding Mercury steady, a smart, even pace... He's conserving, Sarah, he's not letting Davies set the terms!"

The two horses thundered down the dirt street: Ares, a storm of raw power, and Mercury, a study in controlled grace. At the bend near the movie theater, Arthur's voice rose. "Here comes the turn! Davies is fighting to control Ares; he's swinging wide! The warhorse isn't nimble enough! Wait... Price is doing it! He's cutting to the inside! He's taken the lead! Sarah, he's a length ahead!"

Sarah spun back around, her hands clasped to her chest, her eyes wide with a mixture of hope and terror. Eleanor grabbed her arm, her face flushed with excitement. They could see the final stretch now, Price and Mercury a seamless union of muscle and will, holding their slim lead.

"Go, Price!" Sarah screamed, her voice raw with a mother's love, all composure gone. "Faster! Go!"

Arthur Middleton was yelling loudest of all, his voice a booming roar that carried across the landing, "GO, MERCURY, GO! RUN, YOU MAGNIFICENT CREATURE, RUN!"

Eleanor shot him a look and gently elbowed him in the ribs. He glanced at her, then at Sarah's anxious, hopeful face, and a wide grin broke out across his own. He immediately changed his tune, his voice joining the women's. "GO, PRICE! GO!"

Silas just stood with his arms crossed, a slow, proud grin spreading across his face as he watched his friend cross the finish line a triumphant half-length ahead.

Davies, his face a mask of fury and disbelief, pulled Ares to a halt. Price, breathing heavily, slid from Mercury's back and gave the horse a grateful pat on the neck.

He had won not with brute power, but with patience, knowledge, and an unshakeable bond with the animal he rode.

Later, after the crowd had dispersed, Price found Davies tending his horse, movements deliberate. He drew a breath and approached.

"Lieutenant," he said evenly. "I've come to ask for your character reference for The Citadel."

Davies stopped brushing and turned, his face a cold mask. "No."

Price felt the wind in his sails collapse—a dead calm

settling over his hopes—leaving him adrift in a familiar, bitter stillness. He had won the race, but he had lost the war.

He gave a single, tight nod and had just turned to go when Davies spoke again.

"The Colonel spoke to me last night," Davies said, his voice now low and weary. "He asked for an assessment of your character. He also said that whether or not I gave that assessment to you was entirely my decision."

He reached into his jacket and drew out a folded letter. "I wrote it then. It was not... complimentary."

He looked at the paper, then back at Price. "But after that race... a man who can ride like that, who understands a horse... he deserves a chance to prove me wrong."

With a decisive rip, he tore the letter in two and let the pieces fall. "You'll have a new letter by morning," he said crisply. "Don't make me regret this."

It was not an act of friendship but of honor; a grudging acknowledgment of defeat, and a testament to a code that valued skill above pride.

That night, after the cheers had faded and the dust had settled, Price walked Mercury back to the stables. Alone, he swung bareback onto the horse and rode him down the darkened beach.

The surf thundered at his side, a relentless barrage like the artillery he would one day know. Mercury's hooves struck sparks against the packed sand, a brief, fleeting fire against the earth.

Price closed his eyes, feeling the wind tear at his face as

he galloped into an unseen storm—not toward a finish line, but toward a fire-lit horizon he couldn't yet see.

He would not remember the details of that night years later, only the sensation: a race in the wild surf, a pact being sealed between a man, a horse, and a war yet to come.

24

THE TEST

AUGUST 1914

The race had been won, the reference from Davies secured, but the Colonel's warning proved to be the more formidable obstacle. The rest of August was not a celebration; it was a trial by lamplight.

Price sat at the small kitchen table in their cottage, the air thick and still, the kerosene lamp hissing a quiet accompaniment to the relentless calls of katydids. Spread before him were borrowed textbooks: a geometry primer and a daunting, thick volume of *Caesar's Gallic Wars*.

It was a language he did not speak, from a world he did not know. He stared at the pages, his mind, so quick to read the currents of the sea or the spirit of a horse, could find no purchase on the dense blocks of Latin.

Amo, amas, amat. The conjugations were a meaningless puzzle. The geometry was worse—a cold, unforgiving logic of axioms and proofs that felt utterly alien.

He ran a hand through his hair, frustration a tight knot in his chest. He could haul ice for twelve hours, drag a surfboat through sand, and outwit an officer on horseback, but this... this felt impossible. He was the "ice boy" again, staring at a wall he could not climb.

His mother came in, placing a cup of water by his hand. She saw the look on his face, pulled up a chair, and sat beside him. She looked at the jumble of equations on his paper.

"Your father used to say that faith was just studying a map you couldn't understand, but trusting the man who drew it." She tapped the Latin book. "This is just another kind of map, Price. You're smart enough. You just have to learn its language."

She put her finger on the first line of *Caesar*. "Look. *'Gallia est omnis divisa in partes tres.'* Don't see the whole page. Just see the words. *'Gallia'*. What does that sound like?"

"Gaul?" he tried.

"Exactly. *'est'*. 'is'. *'omnis'*. 'all'. Gaul is all... *'divisa'*. "

"Divided?" he offered, the piece clicking into place.

"Into *'partes tres'*. Three parts. See?" she smiled. "You're reading Latin. It's not a wall, Price. It's just a door. You just needed the key. Now, let's try the next line."

He let out a long breath, his mother's steady faith calming his raw nerves. For the rest of the night, she sat with him, her teacher's patience breaking down the complex grammar, turning the impossible text into a story. He turned back to the page, his brow furrowed in concentration. One line at a time.

A week later, after traveling to Charleston to sit for the grueling, day-long examination, he was back on Sullivan's Island. The wait began. He was back on the ice route, his future uncertain, his mind replaying every fumbled equation. The heat felt heavier, the blocks of ice weighed more.

The letter arrived on a Tuesday, delivered by the regular postman. It was an official envelope, thick and imposing, bearing the seal of The Citadel.

He wiped his hands on his trousers before opening it, his heart hammering. He read the words—"We are pleased to inform you of your acceptance..."—and the world, for a moment, went quiet. The letter wasn't just paper. It was a pardon. A key.

He thought of the foreman at the fort, of the injustice of the docked pay, of the endless, sweltering days that stretched before him—a life of hard labor from which he'd seen no escape.

That future, which had felt as solid and unyielding as a granite wall, suddenly had a door. He had passed the test. He was, finally, on his way.

25

THE WATCH - PART I

LATE AUGUST 1914

On his last night on the island, Price found Silas on the dunes, watching the sun dogs in the sky. The tide was out, exposing a wide, shell-strewn flat. A squadron of brown pelicans flew low over the water in silent, disciplined formation.

Farther out, a pod of dolphins surfed the outer breakers, their bodies arcing from the waves in sleek, dark flashes of pure, untamed joy before vanishing into the growing dusk.

For a long time, they sat in a comfortable silence, the rhythmic crash of the waves the only sound.

"So, you're off to play soldier with the fancy boys," Silas said finally, his tone light but his eyes serious. "It's a different kind of ocean you're sailing into, kid."

Price nodded, knowing it was true. "I'll be fine."

"I know you will," Silas said. "But you remember what I taught you about the rip. It ain't just in the water. People have their currents. They'll try to pull you into their way of thinking, their rivalries, their expectations. It can be a strong pull, enough to drown a good man if he's not careful."

He looked at Price, his gaze direct. "Don't fight their currents head-on. You'll just wear yourself out. You just swim parallel. Find your own water. You know who you are, Price. Don't let them make you forget it."

"You know," Silas said, looking at the bottle in his hands. "If you decide you can't hack it with those fancy boys, you're old enough now. I'd put in a word with Captain Adams. The Service could use a man with your salt."

Price thought for a moment of that life—a world of honest labor, of shared risk and the simple, brutal clarity of the sea. A life here, with Silas, where a man's worth was measured by his courage, not his name.

Price slowly shook his head, a small, resolute motion. Thankful for his friend, thankful for the offer.

Silas clapped Price on the shoulder, a firm, final gesture. "Don't you go and drown out there, you hear?"

Price smiled, a genuine, grateful smile. "I won't."

Silas watched him go, a straight-backed figure disappearing into the dusk. For the first time in years, the memory of Coste surfaced not with the sharp sting of guilt, but with a quiet sense of peace.

He hadn't been able to save the young surfman, but he had given this boy the lessons Coste never had the time to learn. He had squared away the line. He turned his gaze back to the sea, his watch now a little less heavy.

PART II: THE CURRENTS

"I took the one less traveled by, And that has made all the difference."

— Robert Frost, "The Road Not Taken"

26

THE GRINDER

SEPTEMBER 1914

The Citadel - Charleston, South Carolina

The parade ground was a furnace. Cadets called it "the Grinder," and it lived up to its name. Heat radiated from the packed earth, and the air was so thick with humidity it felt like breathing water.

The stiff, high collar of his wool uniform was a ring of scratching fire around his neck, and sweat trickled in salty rivers down his spine, pasting the rough fabric to his skin.

He stood in formation, his focus absolute, his world shrunk to the ten feet in front of him and the booming voice of the drill instructor. "...Order, ARMS! Right, FACE!" The movements were becoming instinctive, but the cost was a mind wiped clean of everything but the rhythm of the drill.

During a water break, the cadets scrambled for the blessed shade of the barracks wall. Price leaned against the cool brick in the shade, tilting his canteen to his lips.

That's when he saw it. Cadet Major Randall, a man

whose swagger seemed to take up more space than his body, was mercilessly berating a younger knob named Peterson.

Price desperately wanted to step in, but he could hear Silas's voice in his head, calm and steady as the tide: 'You don't fight the current head-on; you'll just wear yourself out.' Randall was a current of pure poison, and for now, all Price could do was swim parallel and wait for his moment. As a sponsored cadet on trial, Randall would have him expelled immediately.

Peterson was a scrawny boy from the Lowcountry, his face pale and slick with sweat, his eyes wide with a mixture of fear and heat exhaustion. His rifle, a heavy 1903 Springfield, was tilted at a slightly incorrect angle.

"Peterson, do you think this is a debutante ball?" Randall's voice was a low, cruel sneer that carried across the yard. "Is that how you hold a weapon, like a lady holds a teacup? Is that your pinky in the air? Or are you holding it that way because your mother isn't here to hold your limp pathetic little hand?"

Peterson, pale and shaking, tried to correct his posture and his rifle, but his hands fumbled. He looked as if he might faint. Randall stepped closer, his face inches from the boy's. "I will personally see to it that you are ringing the chapel bells for every demerit until Christmas. Do you understand me?"

Just as Randall was about to escalate, a voice cut in from the side. "Sir, with respect, the heat is getting to him. He was on the verge of collapsing a minute ago. Maybe a moment in the shade would prevent a real problem for the medics."

It was Thomas Reed. He stood casually, holding his canteen, his expression deferential but his eyes unwavering.

There was no challenge in his tone, only calm, irrefutable logic.

Randall shot Reed a venomous look, his authority publicly questioned. For a tense second, the air crackled. However, punishing Reed for a reasonable suggestion would make Randall look like a bully. Seeing the logic and avoiding a scene, he sneered. "See that he drinks water," he barked, before turning and stalking away. Reed gave the trembling Peterson a discreet nod before retrieving his canteen.

Later, Price found Reed by the water pump, refilling his canteen with a slow, deliberate motion. The harsh, metallic taste of the sulfur water was a small price to pay for the coolness. "That was a risk you took back there," Price said quietly.

Reed shrugged, not looking up. "Not really. Randall is a sadist, but he's not stupid. A knob collapsing from heatstroke on his watch is a black mark on his record. I just gave him a respectable way out."

He screwed the cap on his canteen and finally looked at Price, his eyes assessing. "Most knobs," he said, "just stare at their boots when a man like Randall starts shouting. You didn't. You were weighing him up." He gave a slight, knowing nod. "You're not one of them."

"No," Price said, the word feeling more true than ever before. "I'm not." "Good," Reed replied. A silent pact was formed in that shared moment. Price finally felt he wasn't entirely alone in this crucible.

27

THE SOCIAL

DECEMBER 1914

The Citadel

The rivalry, once confined to the summer sands of Sullivan's Island, found new and fertile ground within the stone walls of The Citadel.

Lieutenant Davies had made himself a frequent guest at the academy's formal hops and socials, a constant, condescending presence in Price's life. He never missed an opportunity to assert his superiority.

At a formal Christmas social, while Price stood stiffly beside Clara, Davies approached with a proprietary smile. "Chamberlain, you look lovely as always," he said, his eyes sweeping over her gown before turning to Price. "And Hays. I see they've managed to get you into a knob's uniform. A remarkable improvement."

He then turned his back on Price, focusing his full attention on Clara. "I was just telling your father that I've secured a new mount from the cavalry stables. A magnificent thoroughbred. We should ride this Saturday. We could take the old path along the Ashley River, just as we used to."

The words were a deliberate blade, meant to remind Price of a shared history, a comfortable intimacy that excluded him. Price felt Clara's hand tighten on his arm, a small, reassuring gesture. "That's very kind of you, Lieutenant," Clara said, her voice cool. "But Cadet Hays and I already have plans."

Davies' smile tightened for a fraction of a second. "Of course. Another time, then." He then added with a charming but dismissive smile, "A woman of your station has more important things to concern herself with than the company of cadets."

"And what things are those, Lieutenant?" Clara asked, her voice losing its playful edge and taking on a cool, sharp clarity. "The proper arrangement of flowers? The seating chart at a dinner party? I assure you, my mind is capable of more than domestic administration."

The words, sharp and unfamiliar, felt borrowed from the pages of the book hidden between her mattresses—a flash of Wharton's fire in a world that expected only polite embers. Davies' comment, meant to be a charming admonishment, had ignited something.

Price saw it then—a flicker of something, a flame in Clara's eyes, a brief, unguarded glimpse of a fierce intelligence and a deep frustration, before it was instantly masked by the placid, polite smile she had perfected over years of cotillions.

Price realized with a jolt that the charming, witty girl on the porch was a performance, a role she played with masterful skill. And for the first time, he wondered who the real Clara was, and if he would ever be allowed to meet her.

As Davies moved on to flatter another debutante's mother, and Price went to get her champagne, for a fleeting moment, Clara was alone. Her smile, so perfectly practiced, faltered. She looked past the glittering chandeliers and the swirl of pastel gowns to the dark window, seeing only her reflection trapped in the glass.

She felt a familiar, stifling ache—the feeling of a beautiful, perfectly decorated room with no air to breathe. This was the hollowness.

She had been trained to master every room she entered, but tonight something had changed. This world of parlor games and strategic marriages felt less like a life and more like the heavy, golden chains of a campaign that had been carefully managed for her by others.

28

THE GARDEN WALL

SPRING — LATE 1915

Charleston

P rice's life outside the barracks was an education in a different kind of discipline: the world of Charleston society. One sun-drenched Sunday, Price found himself at a lawn-tennis party on the grounds of a sprawling estate south of Broad Street.

The air was thick with the scent of freshly cut grass and the sweet, minty aroma of juleps served in frosted silver cups. Men in crisp white trousers and women in elegant, high-collared dresses moved with an effortless grace, their conversation a low, polite murmur punctuated by the gentle thwack of the tennis ball.

Price, in a borrowed white linen suit that felt both false and impossibly fragile, stood awkwardly near a grand magnolia tree. He watched Clara move across the court, a vision of focused energy. She laughed, a light, carefree sound that carried on the breeze as she scored a point.

She was entirely in her element, navigating the intricate

social currents with the same ease she displayed on the court. For Price, it felt like a foreign country with a language he couldn't speak. The polite smiles directed his way felt like inspections; the small talk about regattas and summer trips to Europe was a vocabulary he didn't possess.

Later, during a break in play, she found him standing alone near the magnolia tree. She followed his gaze across the manicured lawn to the high brick garden walls. "Plotting your escape, Mr. Hays?" she teased, her voice light. Then, more quietly, she added, "Does this world feel terribly small to you sometimes?"

The question hung in the air between them, and Price got the sense she might not be talking about him.

The Charleston Cotillion, the formal presentation of the season's debutantes, was the pinnacle of this alien landscape. Held in the grand, second-floor ballroom of the Hibernian Hall, the ascent to the main event was a trial in itself.

As Price climbed the sweeping marble staircase, he felt a genuine sense of awe. He had never seen such a thing. Light from a massive crystal chandelier glittered on the polished brass, on the silk gowns of the women, and on the gold braid on the uniforms.

This wasn't just a staircase; it was a physical ascent into a world of power and beauty he had only read about. It was seductive, and for a moment, standing beside Clara, he felt a surge of pride. He belonged.

But the feeling changed as quickly as it formed. His gaze followed the flow of people: the city's matriarchs and senior officers held the landing at the top, a fortress of established power. Junior officers and their wives populated the middle, while down at the bottom, cadets and younger knobs waited, looking up with a mixture of aspiration and anxiety.

It was Officers' Row on Sullivan's Island, rebuilt in marble and silk. It was a system of external judgment, of men measuring each other by the shine on their boots and the name on their commission. This climb, he realized, was all surface. It wasn't a path of purpose; it was a performance.

He reached the landing, the air thick with perfume and the sound of the orchestra. Clara took his arm, her touch pulling him back to the present, and led him into the grand ballroom.

Together, they watched as young women in white gowns performed intricate dances and old, mystifying rituals. "Isn't it lovely?" Clara whispered to him, her eyes shining.

Price nodded, but felt a sense of dislocation, as if he were watching a play with himself in it, from far away. The sense of dislocation that began on the staircase had now fully settled on him.

He saw Colonel and Mrs. Chamberlain watching them, whispering, perhaps appraising them. Price felt gratitude, but he also felt the pressure of an obligation he wasn't sure he could ever truly fulfill.

Later that night, they escaped the stifling ballroom for a walk along the Battery, the harbor breeze a welcome relief. Under the soft glow of the gas lamps, the tension in Price's shoulders finally eased.

Here, with the rhythm of the waves against the seawall,

they could almost be the two young lovers who met in the dunes. "You were very handsome tonight," Clara said, taking his arm. "Every girl there was jealous of me."

"I felt like a mule at a thoroughbred race," he admitted, and she laughed. It was in these quiet, honest moments that he felt the deepest connection to her. But as they walked, their conversation turned to the future, and the invisible wall between them reappeared.

Clara spoke of a life in Charleston, where she managed a household, hosted social gatherings, and supported her husband's career as an officer. It was a future she had been raised for, a path as clear and defined as the gardens on the estates they frequented.

Price listened, but he couldn't see his future; this was all so new to him. His dreams of the future crashed when his father died, and he hadn't had time to rebuild them.

29

FIRE AND STORM

LATE 1915

The Citadel

One night, under the arched colonnades of the Citadel quad, Lieutenant Davies, smelling strongly of whiskey, cornered Price in the courtyard. His uniform, usually immaculate, was askew, his tie loosened.

His voice was a low, conspiratorial rasp. "Hays," he began, the name a dismissal of rank. "You think this is a game, don't you? A fairy tale where the pauper wins the princess." He took an unsteady step closer, the bitterness in his eyes raw and unguarded.

"I escorted Clara to her first cotillion. I stood in that grand parlor while her mother fussed with her dress and the Colonel eyed me the way he now eyes you. She isn't some prize to be won."

He leaned in, his voice dropping to a harsh whisper. "She's fire and storm, wrapped in silk and good manners—one moment she's quoting poetry, the next she's plotting a rebellion. She's complicated. And she's loyal to her world, to her father... to the life she knows."

Davies straightened up, a flash of his old arrogance returning, but it was brittle now. "So I'm telling you this once. I know Clara, much longer than you—a complicated girl, that one. Do not be the foolish mill boy that you are. You will not win her in the end."

～

Clara's Letter

My Dearest Price,

Another cotillion has passed. I saw you standing by the French doors, looking out at the night ...

She put the pen down, the words feeling inadequate. She wanted to bridge the distance she felt growing between them, but her world was the only one she had to offer him. She folded the note and, like the others, tucked it away, unsent.

30

JULIA
OCTOBER 1915

Charleston

Price escaped the barracks and sought refuge at the Charleston Library Society on King Street. It was an architectural marvel—a building the likes of which a boy from the Upstate had never seen. Light streamed through tall windows, illuminating a striking black-and-white checkered floor.

One Fall afternoon, he was struggling with a translation of Caesar's Gallic Wars when he became aware of a studied intensity at the next table. A young librarian was bent over a different text, a fragile-looking medieval manuscript, a magnifying glass in one hand. She was so absorbed she seemed to be in another century, her brow furrowed in concentration.

Eventually, she set her work aside with a soft sigh and glanced over, noticing his frustration. "Ah, Caesar," she said with a knowing smile. "Still conquering people two thousand years later, one student at a time. He can be a tyrant in any language. May I?" She gestured to his book. "Sometimes a second pair of eyes can see the path."

He nodded, grateful, and slid the heavy volume across the table toward her. When she spoke, her voice was clear and direct. "He's being deliberately obtuse there," she explained, pointing to the passage. "It's a political move. He's hiding his ambition behind military logistics."

Price found himself intrigued not just by her help, but by the focused passion she so clearly had for the stories hidden in these old books.

He extended his hand. "I'm Price Hays... well, George Price Hays... but everyone calls me Price."

The librarian smiled, a hint of playful mystery in her eyes as she shook his hand. "And I am Julia. Would you like some help?"

Price replied, "Yes," and pointed to a passage on the page. "The bridge. Caesar spends pages on the timber, the pilings, the engineering... it feels so... irrelevant. Just a technical problem."

"That's the point," she said, her voice clear and direct. "He frames his military campaigns as defensive, or as simple technical challenges—like building a bridge. It's how he hides his ambition."

"Hides his ambition?"

"Of course," she said, leaning slightly closer, her voice dropping to a confidential tone. "He's masking his aggression. He writes of logistics, the roads, the siegeworks... It's all ambition wrapped in the language of prudent management. He makes conquest look like an engineering feat. What he's after is the conquest on the other side of the bridge. He rarely writes about that."

Price stared at her, intrigued by her sharp, immediate analysis. His gaze then drifted from the ancient text to a headline in *The New York Times* sitting on a nearby reading table:

LUSITANIA SUNK BY A SUBMARINE, 1,260 DEAD

The words felt unreal, cold—civilians swallowed by the Atlantic.

"Prudent management," Price repeated, his voice hardening as he nodded toward the newspaper. "The Germans are doing the same thing. They claim the Lusitania was a legitimate target because it was supposedly carrying munitions. They're wrapping Emperor Wilhelm's ambitions in Caesar's language of logistics."

Julia followed his gaze, and the academic light in her eyes wasn't just shining; it was burning. "A new emperor," she said, her voice low and fierce, "using an old tyrant's playbook. Sinking a passenger ship of innocent civilians and saying it was somehow justified."

The moment of grim understanding hung in the air between them. For Price, it felt like a sudden chill. This wasn't a history lesson. It was the present. The Roman who wrote this book and the German emperor who sank that ship... they were the same man.

As she helped him decipher the Latin, he found himself listening more to the musical quality of her voice than to the translation. There was a subtle, elegant precision to her pronunciation.

"Forgive me for asking," he said, emboldened by her easy manner. "But your accent... it's not from Charleston, is it? It's very slight."

A spark of genuine pleasure lit her eyes. "You have a good ear, Mr. Hays. Most people don't catch it. My family is French. Moreau."

"Moreau," Price repeated, liking the sound of it.

"*Enchanté de vous rencontrer, Mademoiselle Moreau*"— Pleased to meet you, Miss Moreau.

Julia's smile blossomed into one of genuine surprise and delight. "You speak French, Mr. Hays?"

"It's required at The Citadel," he admitted. "Though I confess I find it more interesting than Caesar's battlefield accounts."

"A cadet with an ear for language is a rare thing indeed," she teased. "My father is Louis Moreau; he keeps a ship-chandlery on East Bay Street. It's a world of its own—the air thick with the smell of hemp rope, tar, and canvas. The sound is the most amazing part: the constant haggling of sailors from around the world, a beautiful tapestry of English, French and West African tongues."

Julia, too, was distracted as she glanced again at the Lusitania headline. She continued, "Since the war began in Europe, Father refuses to provision any ship flying a German flag. He says he will not sell rope to a man who might use it to hang his countrymen."

"A man of principle," Price said with admiration.

"He is," Julia agreed. "Which is why, as a good Catholic, my parents named me for a saint."

Price looked puzzled. "My father was a Presbyterian minister, I basically grew up in a church until I turned sixteen—I've never heard of a Saint Julia."

Julia laughed, a sound so lovely it seemed to fill the intimate space. With a smile in her eyes, she said, "Oh, silly of me—my full name is Helena Julia Augusta Moreau. I was named after St. Helena, Constantine's mother."

Price, a pastor's son, knew the name Constantine but little of his mother. "Saint Helena?"

"The very one," Julia said, her voice softening.

Price asked, "Forgive me, what is she the saint of?"

"St. Helena traveled to the Holy Land and tradition holds she found the True Cross. She was a trailblazer, a woman of great resolve who helped mark a path through trial. The Stations of the Cross—for many, they are a map to endure the impossible."

As she spoke, Price felt a strange resonance, a feeling of being seen not just as a cadet, but as a man on a difficult path. The intensity in her eyes, the way she spoke. He must have looked troubled, for her expression softened further.

"Every man is judged by someone, Mr. Hays. The First Station tells that even Christ was condemned. It is a trial, to be deemed unworthy by the world."

The words struck him, a direct echo of how he had felt after Colonel Chamberlain's initial judgment and dismissal. He felt a sudden, inexplicable chill, thinking of the name of the Station where he'd saved the women, and asked, "Is there a Tenth Station?"

Julia nodded and continued, "The Tenth Station is when He is stripped of His garments. When everything worldly is taken away, leaving only the will to endure. It is a station of profound vulnerability."

She looked at him, her eyes bright with sudden insight. "But it's not only a religious story, Mr. Hays," she whispered.

"It's a story of a man who keeps getting up. It's a map of courage."

He had never heard this tradition spoken of this way—not as a set of rules, but as a series of stations, of trials to be endured.

31

THE EMPRESS
NOVEMBER 1915

Charleston

The next time he saw her, a thick autumn rain was lashing against the tall, arched windows of the library, turning the world outside into a gray, blurred wash. Inside, the air smelled of old paper, leather, and rain-soaked wool.

The library felt like a ship navigating a storm, an ark preserving the stories of a world that seemed determined to tear itself apart.

Price sat at a table, not with a book of tactics, but with a large, linen-backed map of Europe spread before him. The black lines denoted borders, and the red lines showed the advance of the German army on the Western Front.

"It is a daunting thing, isn't it?" a soft voice said beside him. "To see the whole world at war, laid out in neat, clean lines."

He looked up to see Julia. She wasn't smiling in her usual, easy way. Her expression was somber, her gaze fixed on the map with a deep, sorrowful understanding. She pulled a chair from a nearby table and sat, the legs scraping softly against the checkered marble floor.

"My father looks at his shipping charts," she said, her voice a low murmur, "and he sees the U-boats like sharks, circling. He sees the harbors that are closed, the routes that are now a death sentence. It is a map of fear."

She traced a finger over a town near the Somme, a name that had become synonymous with graveyards. "This isn't a map of strategy," she whispered. "It's a ledger of the dead."

"I feel..." Price began, then stopped, searching for the word. "Small. Like none of what we do here matters. Given the horrors that are happening over there." He gestured to the red lines, to the names of French towns where thousands of men were already dying.

Julia was silent for a long moment. Then she said, "Remember the story of St. Helena? The empress I told you about? There is more to her journey. She was an old woman who found a different kind of map when the world believed all the roads were lost."

Price looked at her, intrigued. In the warm glow of the reading lamp, he could see the passion in her eyes, a conviction that felt like the only solid thing in the room. Her presence was a comfort, an anchor for his unsettled mind.

"When St. Helena got to Jerusalem," Julia continued, her voice taking on the cadence of a storyteller, "it was a Roman city. The places of the Passion were gone, deliberately buried by another emperor a century before. On the very spot of the Crucifixion, on Golgotha, they had built a grand temple to the goddess Venus. They had tried to bury the story of sacrifice under a monument to worldly pleasure."

"Helena ordered the temple torn down," Julia continued,

her voice filled with a hushed fire. "And she began to dig. Imagine the faith it took. Her soldiers, her bishops—they must have thought she was a mad old woman, digging in the dirt for a ghost."

He saw it then in his mind: the defiance of an old woman digging for something sacred while the world called her a fool. He knew that feeling—the sting of being judged unworthy, the resolve to prove them wrong.

"But she persisted. And in a cistern, buried deep in the earth, they found them. Three wooden crosses."

"Three?" Price asked, drawn into the story.

"Three," Julia affirmed. "The one Christ was crucified on, and those of the two thieves beside him. But they were just wood. How could they know which was the True Cross?"

She paused, letting the question hang in the air. "The old stories say they brought a dying woman from the city. They touched her with the first cross. Nothing happened. The second, the same. But when the third cross touched her, she was healed, her life given back to her."

"A miracle," Price breathed, the word feeling foreign and yet familiar from his childhood.

Julia looked at him intently, her gaze cutting through the centuries. "It's not a story about the magic of the wood, Mr. Hays. It's a story about how you recognize the truth. The truth doesn't argue with you. It doesn't try to prove itself. It simply gives life. It heals what is broken. That is how Helena knew."

The simple, profound idea settled in Price's heart. He thought of his mother's compass, of his father's decency. He thought of the feeling he had in this library, with her.

"But she didn't just keep it for herself," Julia finished, her voice dropping to a near whisper. "She sent pieces of it to the great cities of the world. And in Jerusalem, she built four great churches, marking the path of the Passion from His birth to His death and His resurrection. She wasn't just building monuments of stone. She was marking a trail. She was leaving signs in the wilderness for every soul that would come after her, lost and looking for a way. She was creating a map."

Price stared at the map of Europe on the table, at its lines of death and division. But he was seeing another map now—a map of endurance, of faith that digs for hope under the rubble of the world's cynicism. He saw an old woman, her back bent but her will unbroken, marking a trail not for an army but for the human heart.

He looked at Julia, at the passion and conviction in her eyes, and felt a sense of awe that had nothing to do with emperors or armies.

"So she found her truth," he said slowly, "and then spent the rest of her life making sure others could find it, too."

"That is what faith is, isn't it?" Julia replied. "Not just finding your way through the storm, but leaving a light on for the next person."

The rain beat a steady rhythm against the glass, but inside the library, in the warm glow of the lamps, Price felt a subtle shift within him. The map on the table was still a map of fear—but as the storm raged outside, he felt the quiet of a harbor settle in his soul. He was no longer looking at it alone.

32

CURRENTS

DECEMBER 1915

Sullivan's Island

T he December air had a crisp edge to it, and the late afternoon sun slanted through the high windows of the Life-Saving Station boathouse, illuminating dust motes dancing in the still air. The massive surfboat rested in its cradle, a silent beast waiting for a storm. The room smelled of fresh varnish and the sharp tang of cleaning oil.

Price sat on an overturned dory, methodically whipping the end of a frayed rope, the repetitive motion a poor anchor for his restless mind. Silas stood at a workbench, meticulously oiling the brass firing mechanism of the Lyle gun, his movements economical and precise.

For a long while, neither spoke. The only sounds were the scrape of Silas's oilcloth on the brass and the rhythmic pull of Price's twine. Silas watched him, a knowing look in his eyes. "That's the third time you've wrapped that line. Your mind's a thousand miles away, kid."

Price sighed, letting the rope go slack in his hands. "Is it that obvious?"

"To me it is," Silas said, setting the firing pin on a clean rag. He leaned against the workbench, his arms crossed. "You've got that look. Like a fish caught between two currents, not sure which way to swim."

The metaphor was so apt that it was startling. Price managed a weak smile. "Something like that."

He hesitated, then the words came out, a confession to the only person he felt could truly understand. "It's... complicated. There's Clara, you know. And her world. Cotillions, lawn parties... it's all fine. She's... she's great, Silas. She's smart, and funny, and she's stood by me. It's just...”

"It's not your world," Silas finished for him, his voice gentle.

“No,” Price admitted. “But her father—the Colonel—he gave me everything, Silas. The Citadel, this uniform. There's no formal engagement, not in writing. But it's a promise everyone expects me to keep. An unspoken one. I owe him. And that makes me feel... promised to her.”

He looked out at the water, the reflection shivering in the tide.

“But then I met someone. A librarian. Julia. When I'm with her, it's different. We just talk. We don't talk about socials or what the Colonel expects. We talk about history. Books. Faith, even. She sees things in a way I've never heard before. When I'm with her, I don't feel like I have to climb or perform. I can just breathe. It feels—” He trailed off, unable to find the right word.

"True?" Silas offered.

Price nodded, a sense of relief and deep peace washing over him. "Yeah. Uncomplicated. It feels true."

Silas was quiet for a moment, absorbing this. Then a slow, mischievous grin spread across his face. "A librarian, huh? She pretty?"

"That's not the point," Price said quickly, a little too quickly.

"It's never the point, but it's always part of the story," Silas chuckled. He sat up, his expression turning to one of mock seriousness.

"Well, this is a serious problem, my friend. A beautiful, smart librarian who talks about real things. Sounds dangerous. I think, as your mentor and protector from treacherous waters, I'd better check her out for myself. You should introduce me."

The suggestion was light, a friendly jest, but it hit Price with an unexpected force. An instinct he didn't recognize—sharp and protective—surged through him.

"Get your own librarian, McGuire," Price said, laughing as he gave Silas a hard, playful shove.

Caught off balance, Silas tumbled from his perch on the workbench and landed with a soft *thump* in a pile of folded tarps. He looked up with a mock wounded expression.

"All right, all right." he said, holding his hands up in surrender, "Just trying to help you steer the ship. But I see you want to navigate these waters alone. Don't come crying to me when you crash your boat on 'Debutante Reef.'"

33

THE MARKET
JANUARY 1916

Charleston

The next Saturday, craving distance from the barracks' dull gray routine, Price walked to the open-air market in Charleston, a chaotic symphony of vendors hawking their wares. This was not the Charleston of polished parlors and piano recitals. Here, the city *breathed*.

He was watching a blacksmith hammer the curve of a wrought-iron gate when he heard a laugh—a clear, musical sound that cut through the noise of the crowd. He turned and saw Julia, her hair tied back with a simple ribbon, haggling with a Gullah woman over a sweetgrass basket.

"Fifty cents is robbery, Miss Rose," Julia was saying in a playful, conspiratorial whisper, her French accent more pronounced than in the library's quiet halls. "My grandmother would faint. I'll give you thirty, and a story for your trouble."

The old woman, her face a beautiful map of wrinkles,

cackled. "A story don't pay for my coal, child. But I'll listen while you count out forty cents."

Julia saw him then, and her face lit with a smile that was pure, unreserved delight. It was a different Julia from the serious scholar of the archives—her eyes danced with mischief.

"Mr. Hays! Perfect timing. You must help me." She held up the basket. "Miss Rose is trying to rob me blind for this. What do you think?"

Price studied it for a moment, the intricate, beautiful patterns, its scent of sweet grass and sunshine. "That is the finest basket I have ever seen."

"See?" Miss Rose declared triumphantly. "The soldier agrees! Now, forty cents, and not a penny less."

Julia sighed in mock defeat, then paid the woman and thanked her for her remarkable creation. As they began to walk away into the main thoroughfare of the market, Julia's expression grew more contemplative.

Price watched it all—the swirl of color, the grace of women balancing crates on their heads, the way white families passed without looking. Julia followed his gaze. "It's a world inside a world, isn't it?" she said quietly. "One we're taught not to see."

He hesitated. "The signs are everywhere, of course. But I remember when I came to the island, on the ferry... there was a sign. A simple rope dividing the benches. 'COLORED.' And this beautiful child behind it, in the soot from the engine—it was the way everyone pretended she wasn't even there that stuck with me."

Julia nodded. "That's Charleston. Lines drawn everywhere, even in the air we breathe." She studied him for a moment. "And what did you do?"

He looked down, embarrassed. "Nothing. I just... saw her. But it didn't sit right."

She smiled, not unkindly. "Seeing is where it starts."

He shifted, then said, "My father would've said the same. He was a minister—not one of the loud ones, but he believed that if you stood in a pulpit, you had to speak the truth. He preached against it—all of it. Said segregation was man's law, not God's. Quoted Paul, Galatians: 'There is neither Jew nor Greek, bond nor free.'" Price's voice softened. "It cost him parishioners. Cost him friends. He never softened it."

Julia looked at him, her expression brightening with recognition. "That takes courage."

He shrugged. "Maybe. Or maybe it was just faith. He thought the world could change if enough people believed it ought to."

She met his eyes. "Then you're your father's son."

As they turned into a more crowded aisle, they saw an elderly Gullah woman struggling to lift a heavy basket of rice onto her stall. Others hurried past, caught up in the market's flow. Without a word, Price moved to help her, taking one side of the heavy basket. Julia immediately took the other. Together, they easily lifted it onto the table.

The woman looked up, her deeply lined face breaking into a wide, grateful smile. "Bless you, children," she said, her voice rich with the Lowcountry cadence. Price and Julia exchanged a brief, understanding glance—a silent acknowledgment of a shared instinct, a small act of decency that felt more real than polite conversation.

For a moment, the noise of the market seemed to fall away—just two young people standing in a city steeped in old divisions, quietly realizing they shared a kind of rebellion that didn't need to be shouted to be real.

Julia tucked her arm through his. "Now," her voice dropping to a low, adventurous tone, "I'm on a secret mission. My father craves the potted shrimp from Mr. Joseph's stand, and he swears no one makes it better. But Mr. Joseph is a terrible flirt. You must pretend to be my stern, overprotective brother so he doesn't try to charm me into buying his entire inventory."

Price found himself laughing. "I'm not sure I can be very stern around you, Miss Moreau."

"Oh, you must try," she insisted, her eyes sparkling. "It's for a noble cause."

For the next hour, she led him through the market's maze. She seemed to know everyone—the fishermen with their silver catches, the farmers with their bright pyramids of produce. She spoke a few words of the Gullah dialect with one vendor, then debated the virtues of French roast versus New Orleans chicory with another.

She moved through this world with a vibrant, confident grace that was entirely different from Clara's practiced social poise. This wasn't a performance; it was life itself.

She stopped at a stall selling benne wafers and pralines, buying a small bag of each and handing him a warm wafer. The nutty, sesame flavor was delicious.

"You see, Mr. Hays," she said, her expression turning serious for a moment, though the laughter never quite left her eyes. "A library holds the stories of the world, but the market... the market is where the stories are still being written. You just have to know how to listen."

As they walked back toward the quieter streets, the energy of the market still buzzing around them, he felt a sense of ease. With her, he wasn't a cadet, a sponsored project, or a boy from a mill town. He was just a man, sharing a stolen, perfect afternoon.

For the first time in months, the war felt distant— another man's story, told on some faraway front.

And the thought of returning to the rigid, ordered world of duty and expectation was a heavier burden than ever.

34

A DIFFERENT KIND OF MAP

FEBRUARY 1916

As the chill of winter deepened, the warm library became Price's refuge. His worries of the future and the weight of others' expectations dissolved the moment he stepped through the grand oak doors.

Here, he was not the Colonel's protégé or Clara's intended; he was simply a man on a path of learning and quiet contemplation.

Occasionally, he would see Julia, and she would make him laugh with some witty remark.

One afternoon, he found her in an alcove, a book of medieval woodcuts open before her. He was quiet, his shoulders slumped with a weariness that went deeper than the endless drills.

"You look like a man carrying a burden," she said quietly, her gaze direct and full of an unnerving perception. She wasn't looking at the man in the uniform, but the man inside.

He couldn't bring himself to tell Julia the feeling that he was betraying Clara every time he spoke with her as a friend. She seemed to understand the unspoken conflict.

"My mother used to say that some burdens are a test of strength," she said, her finger tracing one of the woodcuts. "But the real test isn't whether you carry it; it's what you do when you stumble."

She turned the book toward him. The image was of a man falling under the burden of a heavy cross. "The Third Station: Jesus falls for the first time," she explained. "It's a powerful moment, not because of the fall itself, but because of what comes after. He gets back up. The fall doesn't define him. The rising does. It teaches us that to be human is to fall, but to have faith is to rise again."

Price stared at the image. He thought of his first fall—the public humiliation of dropping the ice at the party. He thought of how he was falling now, internally, under the weight of a life that did not fit. Julia was offering him not a solution, but a perspective. The fall was not the end of the story.

35

THE SUMMER WIND

JUNE 1916

Sullivan's Island

Clara had planned it all, a surprise picnic on a secluded stretch of Sullivan's Island beach, not far from the boneyard of ancient, weathered trees.

She spread a thick woolen blanket over the sand and unpacked a wicker basket, revealing chicken salad sandwiches on soft bread, apples so crisp they shone in the sun, and a bottle of white wine, its glass cool and beaded with condensation.

"A formal inspection, Mr. Hays," she announced, her eyes dancing with a playful light as she smoothed a nonexistent wrinkle on his Citadel uniform. "I must ensure the corps is keeping you in proper form."

Price laughed, the sound easy and unburdened. "And what's the verdict, Miss Chamberlain?"

"Hmm," she said, tapping a finger to her lip in mock seriousness. "Stiff. Far too much starch in the collar and the man wearing it. I prescribe an immediate dose of sunshine and leisure."

She handed him a sandwich and leaned against him, her head resting on his shoulder as they looked out at the gentle surf.

In moments like this, the suffocating world of cotillions and formal parlors vanished, and she was simply Clara, the girl he'd met in the dunes.

"This is nice," he said. "Thank you."

"I know this new life... the uniform, the expectations... it wears on you sometimes. I see it in your eyes. I thought I'd rescue you for an afternoon." She didn't press, and he was grateful for it.

She had a way of seeing the storms within him without needing to name them.

They ate in comfortable silence, to the sound of the waves and the cry of a distant gull. After a while, Clara asked:

"What was your father like, Price? You never talk about him."

The question caught him off guard. He swallowed, the sandwich suddenly dry in his mouth. He looked at her, at the genuine, open curiosity in her eyes, and found himself wanting to answer.

"He was... a good man," he began, the words feeling small and inadequate. "A pastor. He had this laugh that could fill the whole church. He taught me how to fish in the Reedy River. He'd stand there for hours, so patient, showing me how to cast, how to feel the tug on the line."

A happy memory surfaced, and for a moment, the grief receded. "One time, the wind was blowing so hard my line kept getting tangled in the reeds. I was ready to call it a day.

But he just smiled and put his hand on my shoulder and said, 'You can't fight the wind, son. You just have to learn its shape and cast with it.'"

The warmth of the memory faded from his eyes, replaced by a sudden, sharp sorrow. "I was 15." His voice grew thick. "We were supposed to go up to the Highlands that next summer. He was going to teach me how to tie flies, how to read a trout stream. He had it all planned..."

He stopped, unable to continue. A raw, familiar ache seized his chest. It wasn't just the loss of his father; it was the loss of all the days that were supposed to come, the lessons never taught, the conversations never had.

A wave of grief, sudden and powerful as a rip current, pulled him under. He squeezed his eyes shut, a single tear escaping and tracing a path through the dust on his cheek.

He felt a gentle pressure as Clara took his hand, her fingers lacing through his. She didn't offer empty platitudes or tell him it was all right.

She moved closer, wrapping an arm around his shoulders, and held him. She rested her head against his, a silent, unwavering presence against the storm inside him. And in holding him, a single, disloyal thought surfaced: the safe, sensible future her father had planned for them felt like a profound betrayal of this raw, honest moment.

She squeezed his hand, a firm, steady pressure. "What does your friend Silas say? You can't fight the rip?" she whispered, her voice soft. "I'll always be here for you, Price—no matter the ferocity of the tide or the storm."

He turned into her embrace, his shoulders shaking with a silent sob he hadn't realized he'd been holding back for years. And in the solid warmth of her arms, he felt a sense of peace.

She wasn't trying to save him from the current; she was holding onto him until it passed. In that moment, he felt an overwhelming surge of love for her, a certainty so powerful it felt like the only solid ground in a world of shifting tides.

He was anchored to this remarkable, witty, and deeply kind woman not by duty or expectation, but by a bond of unwavering grace—a safe harbor in any storm.

36

THE LONG GAME

OCTOBER 1916

The Citadel

The gaslights of the mess hall cast long, dancing shadows on the walls. Price sat with Thomas Reed, the murmur of a hundred cadet conversations a low hum around them.

Price was quiet, his mind still tracing the elegant lines of a poem Julia had shown him earlier that day. Reed, however, was focused on a different kind of text. He was studying the room.

"See him?" Reed said, nodding subtly towards a table near the front where a group of senior cadets held court. "Cadet Captain Morrison."

Price glanced over. Morrison was holding forth, a small circle of cadets laughing a little too loudly at his story. "He seems... loud," Price observed.

"He's a fool," Reed said, his voice a low, clinical assessment. "But he's a useful fool. I spent the last week tutoring him in military history."

Price smirked. "I heard him telling a knob that Hannibal stormed Rome with a thousand war elephants."

Reed let out a short, humorless laugh. "That was *after* my tutelage. Before I started, he thought Hannibal was a brand of canned ham from Georgia. He's learning. Slowly. But he serves a purpose." He gestured subtly with his fork.

"His father is Senator Morrison. The Senator's recommendations for the summer training cadres carry significant weight. By tutoring his son, I'll secure a summer post as an aide at Fort Monroe. That assignment will put me in the room with the senior staff officers on the East Coast."

Price frowned. "But you're one of the smartest in the corps. You should be leading a Battalion, at the very least."

"And get stuck in some backwater infantry drill for three months?" Reed countered, a flicker of impatience in his eyes. He thought of his father, a man who had built a textile mill from nothing, whose calloused hands had been a source of quiet shame at his first Charleston cotillion. His father's last letter was still tucked in his footlocker, the words practically memorized: "*A general's star is a currency they cannot refuse, son. Make them respect the name Reed.*"

Reed leaned forward, his gaze intense. "Price, this isn't about fighting battles. It's about being in the right room, shaking the right hands. The war in Europe is going to last for years. When we get in, and we will, the men who have the generals' ears will be the ones who write their own tickets."

Reed looked from the calculating sharpness in his eyes to the oblivious arrogance of Cadet Captain Morrison. "This is a long game. You play for the next move, not the one right in front of your face."

37

THE GRAY FORTRESS
OCTOBER 1916

West Point, New York

T he journey north was a revelation. Price had never been farther from South Carolina than the Georgia training camps, and the sheer scale of the country unfolding from the train window was astonishing.

The world grew denser, faster, the towns bleeding into one another until the magnificent, terrifying maw of New York City swallowed them. For a day, they were tourists in a city that felt like the capital of a foreign empire, a place of dizzying heights and a ceaseless, thrumming energy that made Charleston feel like a sleepy village.

But their true destination lay up the Hudson River, a place that was in its own way more imposing than any skyscraper: The United States Military Academy at West Point.

Colonel Chamberlain had been invited to deliver a lecture to the senior cadets on the modernization of coastal artillery, a lecture centered on the strategic importance of the Endicott Program fortifications, such as those at Fort Moultrie.

It was a subject he spoke of with the passion of a zealot, and he had insisted Price accompany him and Clara. "You're the future of the Army, Hays," he had said. "It's time you saw the heart of the beast."

The heart of the beast was a fortress of gray stone perched above a dramatic bend in the river, exuding an aura of inviolable history and tradition. It made The Citadel, with its familiar southern humidity and regional pride, seem like a prep school.

Here, the air felt different—colder, sharper, imbued with the power of a national destiny. The cadets marching on the parade grounds—The Plain, as it was called—moved with a crisp, unified precision that spoke of generations of command.

The lecture hall was a cavernous amphitheater of dark wood and richly painted portraits. Price and Clara sat in the visitors' gallery as hundreds of cadets filed in.

When Colonel Chamberlain took the lectern, his voice echoed with authority. He spoke of the engineering marvels that were transforming the wage of modern war, but then his tone shifted, becoming sharp and urgent.

"Cadets, this is not a history lesson," his voice boomed. "This is a warning. Two months ago, the German submarine U-53 brazenly surfaced in Newport, Rhode Island, paid a courtesy call to an American destroyer, and then, just beyond our territorial waters, proceeded to sink five Allied ships. The enemy is not waiting for a declaration of war. They are at our gates. The fortifications we build, the guns we man... they are the only thing standing between a defenseless coast and an enemy that respects no flag but its own!"

A wave of murmurs went through the cadets, followed by a sudden, sharp burst of applause that grew into a roar.

Clara's eyes shone with pride. But she was also aware of the sea of young, handsome faces looking up at her father. She leaned toward Price, her voice a playful whisper against his ear. "It's like a room full of statues. All perfectly carved for one purpose. They're magnificent."

Price forced a smile, but a strange, unfamiliar emotion coiled in his gut. It was a sting. It wasn't inferiority, it was something else. He watched the cadets and their confident bearing—their place at the absolute center of the American military. They were the chosen ones, the future leaders of the nation, products of an institution that had produced both Generals and Presidents.

Afterward, they walked a winding path along the cliffs, the Hudson a wide, brown-gray swath below. The autumn air was crisp with the scent of burning leaves. Clara slipped her arm through Price's.

"Did you see their faces when Father spoke of the U-boats? They were ready to march out of the room and fight them on the beaches." She sighed, a sound of pure contentment, and gazed across the river at the magnificent Gilded Age estates dotting the opposite shore.

"Can you imagine, Price? Waking up to that beautiful view every morning. That could be us in the future." She gestured across the river. "Those families—the Vanderbilts, the Roosevelts—they don't just host parties. They shape policy. Their wives and daughters... they're not decorating houses. They're running charities, influencing politics, marching for the vote. That is being at the center of the world."

Price looked not at the distant mansions, but at her, at the way the wind caught a stray strand of her hair. He was anchored to the present—happy just with her on his arm, the sharp scent of woodsmoke on the wind, the satisfying crunch of his shoes on the gravel path.

"It's beautiful right here, right now, though," he said, trying to pull her back to him.

"What about you, Clara?" he asked, turning to her. "Not the life your father wants, or what Charleston society expects. What do you want? What does our future look like?"

The question, so simple and direct, stole her breath. For a heart-stopping second, the truth rose in her throat, a rebellion she had never dared to voice. *Tell him. Tell him you dream of a lecture hall at Vassar, not just a parlor in Charleston. Tell him you want to debate policy, not just seating arrangements. Tell him you want a partner, someone who will be on that stage and help change the world.*

But the words caught, trapped behind the perfect, polite mask she had been trained her whole life to wear. Here, in the very fortress of her father's world, the weight of his expectations was too heavy. The courage failed her. Her gaze drifted back across the river to the grand estates.

"Oh, of course it is beautiful here," she agreed, her voice regaining its light, practiced tone. "But over there... that's a different kind of beautiful, isn't it? A kind of... life where anything is possible."

She didn't—or couldn't—answer his question about their future. Instead, she reframed it around the world's changing currents. "The war in Europe... it feels like it's getting closer every day, Price. If America is drawn in, men like you will be needed to lead. When you become an officer, think of the possibilities! Washington? The War College? Father says a man like you will be able to write his own ticket."

He heard the assumption in her words—that his goal was a fast climb up the same ladder. "I don't know, Clara," he said honestly. "I just want to be a man my father would have been proud of. A good man."

"Of course," she said, but her tone was subtly dismissive, as if he'd given a child's answer to an adult's question. "But a good man with influence can do so much more. Don't you see? That's the real battle."

He looked from the stone palaces of the Vanderbilts and Morgans, high atop the cliff across the river to Clara. The distance between them wasn't just about their different upbringings. It was the impossible gulf between the high altitude she sought and the level ground he knew in his heart.

Standing beside the woman he loved, in the institution that represented the pinnacle of the life he was supposed to want, Price felt a loneliness.

The Hudson wind stung his cheeks, but it smelled of rain and smoke—real things.

On the train ride south, Price sat by the window, watching the world blur past. Clara was beside him, reading a novel, while the Colonel, in a seat across from them, feverishly wrote letters.

In the train car, the rhythmic clatter of the wheels on the track was a steady, hypnotic beat, pulling him farther from the gray fortress on the Hudson and deeper into his thoughts.

He watched the landscape transform in reverse. The grand estates and dense industrial towns gave way to rolling hills and open fields.

The electric lights of the northern cities faded, replaced by the scattered, warm glow of farmhouses tucked into the darkening countryside. With each mile, he felt the tightening of his posture begin to unwind, the performance of the last few days falling away.

This was a world he understood. The furrowed fields, the smoke curling from a distant chimney, the silhouette of a lone oak against the twilight sky—it was a landscape that asked nothing of him. It didn't measure his rank or his prospects. It was simply there, honest and solid.

He was still the same man who loved the woman sitting beside him, who felt a profound debt of gratitude to her father. But the trip north had illuminated something in him.

He was more comfortable in places that didn't cost anything—the dunes with Silas, the porch with his mother, the aisles of a stable. It was the same quiet authenticity he'd found in the library with Julia, or the bustling honesty of the market. The life Clara dreamed of, a life at the "top of the world," felt like a stage on which he would always be playing a part.

As the train rumbled over the Santee River in the pre-dawn light, the air through the open window changed, growing thick and humid, carrying the familiar scent of pine and damp earth.

He was returning to the place he was from, but he knew, with an aching certainty, that the man on this train was not the same one who had traveled north.

38

THE UNIFORM

OCTOBER 1916

Charleston

The feeling of dislocation, once a whisper on Sullivan's Island, was now a constant, low roar. It was a weariness that felt most acute at the St. Cecilia Ball, the pinnacle of Charleston's social season.

He climbed the grand Hibernian Hall staircase, but the magic he had once felt was gone. The glittering light no longer seemed to land on "power and beauty," but on the "whisperers and watchers" lining the steps, their polite smiles feeling like inspections.

At the top of the landing, the "judges"—the city's matriarchs and patriarchs—waited, their approval the prize for a flawless performance. He felt the weight of his uniform. This was not a party; it was a gauntlet. With each step up the marble, his spirit felt as if it were climbing down, sinking into a hollow ache of performance.

He stood by the wall of the grand ballroom, watching

Clara move through the crowd, a queen in her court. She was radiant, laughing as she spoke with a handsome young officer from a prominent Charleston family. She was entirely in her element. He was an actor who had forgotten his lines.

"You're a thousand miles away," she said, appearing at his side with two glasses of champagne. Her smile was warm, but her eyes were searching.

"Just tired," he lied. "The drills have been brutal."

She accepted his excuse, but he saw a flicker of doubt in her eyes. She put her arm through his, a gesture of comfort and also ownership. "Come," she said, "I want you to meet Senator Allston. His nephew has just been accepted at West Point. You two will have so much to talk about."

Price shook the Senator's hand, forcing a smile. The man's palm was smooth and soft, a hand that had never known a callus from a tool or a rein. It was the hand of a man who lived in a hollow world of performance, of whispered deals and social rank.

In that moment, Price saw the system for exactly what it was. Clara, at least outwardly, was thriving in this world, moving with a confident grace. But he couldn't shake the memory of the flicker of fire in her eyes at Christmas, or her holding back and hesitating to answer his question above the Hudson River.

Was this her, or just a performance she had perfected? The thought that he might not know the real Clara—or that the real Clara was a willing part of this hollow world— unsettled him almost as much as the senator's soft hands.

He remembered Silas's words: *You don't fight the currents head-on. You swim parallel.*

But surrounded by the powerful tide of Charleston society, he felt as if he were being pulled out to sea, a world away from the free, real sanctuaries he had found—the quiet truth of the library, the bustling life at the market, the simple elemental beauty of the beach. He felt like a traitor, not to Clara, but to himself.

39

LAMP LIGHT

NOVEMBER 1916

A few days later, Price went to the library. The main reading room was nearly empty, the only sounds the soft hiss of the gas lamps and the whisper of turning pages.

He found Julia in the archives. She was bent over a large, vellum map of the Carolina coast, dated 1775. A single lamp cast a pool of golden light on the table, illuminating the delicate, spidery script and faded coastlines.

"Look at this," she said, her voice a low murmur that seemed woven into the room's stillness. She didn't look up, having sensed his presence. "They thought the Santee River was a direct passage to the west. An artery to a whole new world."

He moved to stand beside her, so close he could feel the warmth radiating from her shoulder. He found himself looking not at the map, but at the way the lamplight caught the stray wisps of her dark hair, turning them into a halo.

"They were wrong, of course," she continued, her finger tracing an imagined path through the wilderness. "But you can't help but admire the hope in it. The belief that if you just follow the line, you'll find your way. *C'est un chemin d'espoir,*" she whispered, her French a soft breath in the stillness. "It's a path of hope."

Her hand, elegant and pale against the ancient paper, was only an inch from his. She looked up, and the academic light in her eyes softened into something else, something personal and deeply stirring.

The quiet of the archive deepened, becoming an intimate space that held only the two of them. He saw her glance down at his lips, a fleeting, almost imperceptible motion that sent a jolt of pure electricity through him.

Slowly, instinctively, he began to lean in, the pull between them as undeniable as gravity. She met his gaze, her face tilting upward, a shared longing clear in her eyes. The space between them shrank, charged and alive. He could smell the warm scent of sandalwood and old books on her skin—it was the fragrance of truth, of solace, and he was drowning in it.

But just as their lips were about to meet, the image of Clara's trusting face flashed in his mind—bright and clear as a photograph, her smile unwavering. A wave of guilt, sharp and cold as a bayonet, pierced him. He stopped, pulling back with an almost imperceptible shake of his head. The fragile, perfect moment was shattered.

A flicker of hurt, quickly masked, crossed Julia's face. Her gaze dropped back to the map, her shoulders straightening almost imperceptibly. When she spoke, her voice was carefully neutral, betraying nothing of the wreck that had just occurred. "It's a fragile thing, a map," she said. "Easy to misread."

Price couldn't find any words, his throat tight with the

things he couldn't say. He felt the crushing weight of his divided heart.

In this book-filled sanctuary, he wasn't the sponsored cadet or the hero-in-waiting. He was a man caught between two maps, drawn to two different shores, and he was terrified that in trying to navigate both, he was losing his way entirely.

When they parted at the door, she left the lamp in the west window burning. "For late readers," she said, her smile soft in the glow. He felt the warmth on the sidewalk long after he'd gone.

40

THE SACRAMENT

NOVEMBER 1916

The large oak door of St. Mary's on Hasell Street closed behind Julia, muffling the city's fearful silence and replacing it with the cool, hallowed air of the nave. The scent of old incense and beeswax candles was a comfort, the light filtering through the stained glass windows a kaleidoscope of muted jewels on the stone floor.

She needed a sanctuary, a place of stone and silence to hold the immensity of her feelings after Price had pulled away. And, she needed forgiveness.

She slipped into one of the dark, ornate wooden confessionals that stood like solemn sentinels along the wall, the wood worn smooth by the hands and whispered prayers of generations of penitents.

"Bless me, Father, for I have sinned. It has been one month since my last confession."

She recited her minor transgressions, her voice a low murmur in the stillness. When she finished, the priest's kind but firm baritone voice came through the screen. "Is there anything else troubling your soul, my child?"

Julia hesitated; the words caught in her throat. "Father," she began, her voice barely a whisper, "I have allowed my heart to feel... affection for a young man. A cadet. He is good and honorable. But he is a Presbyterian. And he is spoken for."

The silence that followed was heavy with unspoken law. "Ah," the priest sighed. "My child, the Church does not forbid love, but it commands us to guard our faith. You know of the *Ne Temere* decree. To marry a non-Catholic is a grave matter, requiring a dispensation from the Bishop himself. For this to be granted, you would have to promise, before God, to raise your children in the Church, and he would have to agree not to interfere."

"But Father," her voice filled with a reverent but unshakeable conviction, "I could never ask that of him. His father was a Presbyterian minister. His faith is the foundation of who he is. To ask him to stand aside as his children are raised in a faith that is not his own... it would be a violation of his honor. I cannot do that to him."

The faint scent of incense lingered in the dark wood of the confessional. The priest was silent for a long moment, the gravity of her words settling in the confined space.

When he spoke again, his tone was softer, laced with a sorrowful gravity. "My child, this path doesn't just sever you from the grace of the sacraments—you will be excommunicated—*latae sententiae*—automatically. It severs you from the family that brought you to God. Think of your parents. Think of your mother, Hélène, a devout woman. What will she tell her friends when her own daughter cannot receive the Eucharist beside her? Can you picture her there, in her pew at St. Mary's, Sunday after Sunday?" He paused, his final words a quiet image of the true cost. "Kneeling alone."

Clarity pierced through with dread. She felt her hand instinctively clutch the small crucifix she wore. For Julia, the choice was clear—the honor of the man she loved was far greater than the Church's rules.

The cost of choosing Price, she now understood, meant a very public exile from the Catholic Church, a painful separation from the community and her family life that revolved around it.

"Pray on it, my child," the priest's voice urged gently.

"I... I will, Father," she whispered.

Julia stepped out of the confessional's heavy darkness, not into the bright street, but into the nave of the Church. She slipped into a familiar pew, the polished wood worn smooth by generations of prayer, and knelt.

A wave of doubt, cold and sharp, washed over her. *A map is a fragile thing,* she thought, the memory of her words in the library now a painful echo. *Easy to misread.* Had she misread everything?

Had she mistaken a shared intellectual spark for a path of hope? The honorable thing, the virtuous path, would be to step aside, to leave him to the life he was promised.

Her prayer was not for guidance, but for strength. Her gaze drifted to the carved stations lining the walls, the map of suffering she knew so well. It was the Fourth Station that held her: *Jesus meets His Mother.*

In the sorrowful faces carved into the old wood, she saw not divine tragedy, but a profoundly human one—a mother's unwavering love in the face of her son's certain sacrifice.

She thought of her mother, of the pain her choice would inflict, a fresh wave of grief washing over her. Mary could not take the cross from her son; she could only offer her presence, a fortress for his soul.

Julia knew—if a path ever opened up with Price—it would mean exile from her family, her church, her friends.

She rose from the pew, her prayer for strength answered not with a sign, but with resolve. The day might never come, and the man she loved might never know the depth of her feelings for him.

Until then, she alone would silently bear this cross for him—a sacrament hidden within her heart.

41

***

THE DIVIDE

LATE 1916

Price felt like he was living two different lives. On a weekend afternoon, he'd sit in a parlor with Clara and her mother, nodding through conversations about her sister's wedding. The talk of seating and silver patterns was as far away from the mill town as he had ever been. He found himself smiling and playing the part of the heroic young officer.

The next weekend, he went to the library, where an hour spent with Julia, arguing over a line of poetry, felt more real than anything in his life. At the library, there were no performances, just a search for understanding without pretense.

Late one Sunday, Price returned to the barracks, the scent of Clara's perfume still clinging to his uniform, his mind a turbulent sea. Reed was at his desk, writing a letter home by the light of a single lamp.

He looked up as Price entered, taking in his friend's tormented expression."Another successful campaign on the Charleston front?" Reed asked, his tone gentle.

Price sank onto his cot and ran a hand through his hair. "I feel like a traitor, Tom."

"To which side?" Reed asked shrewdly.

Price had no answer. He just looked at his friend, the question hanging in the air between them, a perfect summation of his second, deeper fall.

42

THE HARBOR

JANUARY 1917

Charleston

The winter chill had driven the cadets indoors, turning the barracks into a close, damp space thick with the smell of wet wool and the low murmur of a hundred restless men.

The air was suffocating, each breath a reminder of the walls that kept them within. For Price, the library was no longer a refuge; it was a necessity, the only place he could find room to think.

He found Julia in a corner of the main reading room, a thick volume of Thucydides' *History of the Peloponnesian War* open before her.

The gas lamps hissed and sighed, casting a warm, golden light on the dark wood of the tables. She looked up as he approached, a welcoming smile that seemed to push back the gloom.

"Escaping the fortress, Mr. Hays?" she asked, her voice a low, pleasant murmur.

"Trying to, Miss Moreau," he said, taking the seat opposite her. "The walls feel a little closer on days like this."

He had come with a purpose.

For weeks, a question had been turning over in his mind, a piece of military history he couldn't reconcile. "I was reading about the Battle of Shiloh," he began. "The first day was a disaster for Grant. He was caught completely by surprise, nearly driven into the river. By all accounts, he should have retreated."

"But he didn't," Julia finished, her interest piqued. She closed her book. "He held his ground. And on the second day, with reinforcements, he won."

"Exactly," Price said, leaning forward. "Every textbook, every instructor, preaches the virtue of the orderly withdrawal. To hold a position when your flank is turned and you're being overrun... it's considered suicide. So why did he stay? What did he see that no one else did?"

Julia was quiet for a long moment, her finger tracing the spine of her book. "Perhaps he wasn't looking at the map of the battlefield," she said thoughtfully. "Perhaps he was looking at the map of his army's spirit."

Price frowned. "I don't understand."

"A retreat, even an orderly one, is a confession of defeat," she explained. "It breaks a soldier's spirit. Grant had an army of volunteers, not professional soldiers. They were held together by morale, not just by discipline. To retreat might have saved them from the battle, but it might have lost him the army. He understood that sometimes, the will to fight is the most important ground to hold. He was a student of the human heart as much as of strategy."

Her insight was a revelation. Price had been studying the

battle as a tactical problem, a matter of lines on a map. Julia saw it as a human drama, a test of will.

"My father," Julia continued, her voice softening, "he says that every man has a harbor inside him, a place of conviction he cannot abandon, no matter how high the tide. For Grant, that harbor was his belief in his men. To abandon it would have been to let them drown."

Price looked at her and felt the same quiet, unwavering stability that the granite rock by the Reedy River had given him as a boy. It was the stillness of a harbor he had not known he was seeking.

They spoke for an hour as the rain lashed against the tall windows, their conversation a quiet harbor of its own.

He saw in her not just a formidable intellect, but a deep and profound empathy, a way of seeing the world that went beyond facts and figures to the very heart of things. It was a language he understood.

When the clock in the hall chimed the hour, he knew he had to leave. "Thank you, Julia," he said, the use of her first name feeling both natural and momentous. "You've given me a lot to think about."

"That's what librarians do—you're very welcome Mr. Hays," she replied, her smile holding a warmth that stayed with him long after he had stepped back out into the cold, gray rain.

43

WINTER LETTERS
JANUARY — FEBRUARY 1917

T he winter of 1917 was a season of writing. The cold, damp, rainy chill that settled over Charleston kept most cadets confined to the barracks during their free hours, turning the mail call into the day's most antici-pated event.

For Price, it was a lifeline, a connection to the many sepa-rate worlds he now inhabited.

My dearest Clara,

The drills on the Grinder are relentless, but in the quiet of the barracks, when the bugle has sounded its last call, I find my thoughts drifting back to the summer.

The air here is cold and smells of coal smoke, a poor substitute for the salt breeze on Sullivan's Island. Tell your father I am applying myself to his faith in me. And, thank your mother for the tin of cookies.

I spend many nights studying by lamplight, though I confess the glow is hardly as memorable as the one in your father's study.

I hope this letter finds you well and that your family is in good spirits.

> *Yours,*
> *Price*

My dearest Son,

Greenville is under a blanket of frost. The mill whistle seems louder in the cold air.

Mr. McCullough sends his regards; he says the livery isn't the same without you and that the horses miss your steady hand.

I pray for you every night, that you are warm and safe. I know you are making your father proud, but don't forget the compass he gave you. It is more important than anything in this world.

I am sending along a tin of ginger cookies. I hope they are not all crumbs by the time they reach you. Do not let the other boys eat them all.

> *All my love,*
> *Mom*

Price,

Heard you're learning how to march in straight lines with the fancy boys. Hope they're teaching you something useful.

We had a drill the other day with the Lyle gun and young Burnham (a new recruit, green as seagrass) nearly took out the watchtower. The Captain was not pleased.

The winter tides have been rough, but the sea is quiet otherwise. No sign of any German predators.

How's that librarian? Has she taught you any new words?

Don't forget how to swim the rough seas, kid. I have a feeling you'll need that lesson more where you are than where I am.

Stay salty,

Silas

From the Journal of Julia Moreau,

Winter has closed in on the library. The rain on the tall windows feels like a constant whisper. A young cadet came in today, shivering, asking for a translation of a French letter from his Uncle.

It made me think of Mr. Hays. I wonder if he is warm, if he remembers our conversations. I find myself praying for him, that he finds his chemin d'espoir.

It is a foolish thing, to pray for a man who belongs to another.

But the heart is not always logical.

44

THE CALL

FEBRUARY — APRIL 1917

The War arrived first as a visible scar in the harbor of Charleston.

In February, the crew of the German freighter SS *Liebenfels*, trapped in Charleston since the War began, scuttled their ship to block the channel, a final, defiant act of sabotage.

The half-submerged wreck was a constant reminder that the distant conflict was creeping closer.

In March, the last fragile arguments for neutrality were swept away in a tidal wave of public outrage.

Price was walking across the Grinder when he saw a crowd of cadets huddled around a single copy of *The News & Courier*, their voices a low, angry buzz.

He pushed closer and saw the headline, splashed in giant, accusatory letters:

ZIMMERMANN TELEGRAM REVEALS GERMAN PLOT

"Can you believe the audacity?" Cadet Peterson spat, jabbing a finger at the paper. "Promising Mexico our land! Texas, Arizona, New Mexico! As if it's theirs to give."

"It's a British trick," another cadet countered, his voice laced with skepticism. "They intercepted it, they translated it, they fed it to us. They've been trying to drag us into their war for years. How do we know it's not a forgery?"

A heated argument erupted. But then Thomas Reed, who had been reading silently over their shoulders, spoke, his voice cutting through the noise with calm authority.

"It's not a forgery," Reed said simply. "Zimmermann himself admitted it. It was in a secondary report on the wire this morning. He confirmed he sent it."

A stunned silence fell over the group. The admission of authenticity changed everything.

It was no longer a question of British propaganda. It was a direct, undeniable act of German aggression against the United States. The distant European squabble had just landed on their doorstep.

"My God," Peterson whispered. "Then it's real."

"It was always real," Reed said, his eyes dark with a meaning that went beyond the day's news. "Some of you just refused to see it."

The crowd dispersed, their debates replaced by a grim, unified understanding.

The threat was no longer an abstract headline. It was here. And they would be the ones sent to answer it.

In April, when President Wilson's call for a declaration of War finally came, it felt less like a choice and more like an inevitability.

On every street corner, newsboys shouted—'War! America declares War!'—through the humid air. The headlines screamed from the page:

PRESIDENT CALLS FOR WAR DECLARATION, STRONGER NAVY, NEW ARMY OF 500,000 MEN

500,000 wasn't a number; it was a summons.

The news collapsed Price's world. Every abstract question of his life was now moot. He would receive an accelerated commission. He would be sent to France.

And he understood, with a cold certainty, that like the millions of soldiers who had already died in the War, he might not come back.

45

HER WAR
APRIL 1917

With Price's commission and the probability of his deployment to France, the war ceased to be a distant headline for Clara. It became a personal, terrifying reality.

The world of lawn parties and cotillions felt frivolous, almost insulting, in the face of what he was about to endure. A sense of helplessness gnawed at her, a feeling she had never known in her carefully managed life.

She found her purpose, as many women of her station did, in the patriotic whirlwind that swept through Charleston.

She saw the transformation on the streets, where young men in ill-fitting new uniforms crowded the sidewalks, their youthful faces a mixture of bravado and fear.

Her mother, a formidable organizer in the city's social circles, was appointed head of the local Liberty Loan drive, and Clara became her most ardent lieutenant.

She discovered she had a talent for it. Standing on a makeshift stage in Marion Square, her voice, usually reserved for polite parlor conversation, rang out with a passion that surprised everyone, including herself.

"Every bond you buy is a bullet in the barrel of a rifle!" she'd call out, her eyes scanning the crowd. "Every dollar is a shield for a son, a brother, a husband! It is a promise to our boys overseas that they are not fighting alone!"

She was magnificent. Men in the crowd, captivated by her beauty and fire, emptied their pockets.

She moved from rallies to private parlors, leveraging her family's name to secure massive pledges from Charleston's wealthiest merchants.

It was a different kind of battlefield, one of persuasion and patriotism, and she was a natural commander.

She was fighting the war in the only way she knew how, using the tools of—her name, her social grace, her influence —as weapons. She was doing her part.

She was helping Price win the war.

46

DIFFERENT PATHS

APRIL 1917

The Citadel

The day the commissions were posted was one of controlled chaos. Cadets crowded the main bulletin board, their futures—and perhaps the length of their lives—pre-determined by simple black ink on white paper.

Price found his name easily: Second Lieutenant George P. Hays, assigned to the 10th Field Artillery, 3rd Division. He read the unit designation again. *10th Field Artillery*.

For a reason he couldn't name, the number felt significant, like a marker on a path he was only just beginning to walk. It was an active combat unit, already preparing for deployment to France. A surge of grim purpose went through him. This was it.

He found Thomas Reed packing his trunk, his movements neat and efficient. Reed's uniform was already different. Pinned to his collar was the insignia of an aide-de-camp.

"Congratulations, Tom," Price said, leaning against the doorframe. "Saw you were assigned to General Bell's staff."

"Thank you," Reed said, a thin, satisfied smile on his face. He folded a pair of perfectly polished boots and placed them in the trunk. "It's a fine opportunity. The General is being tasked with organizing the training divisions stateside. It will be a logistical challenge of immense importance."

Price was silent for a moment. A logistical challenge. Stateside. While men were being shipped to the trenches. "You won't be going to France, then."

Reed finally looked at him, his expression unreadable. "Not at first. My talents are best used here, in the planning stages," Reed said, but then he paused, his gaze turning serious.

"Price, have you *read* the reports from Verdun? Not the headlines—the numbers. This isn't battle; it's slaughter. They call the trenches the Field of Honor. But it's a butcher's block. And I have no intention of laying my neck on it."

He looked up at Price, his expression softening. "This isn't a choice about ambition; it's my only chance to survive. My weapons are my words. I can't shoot, I can't ride, I can't fight. Morrison's father gets me a seat at the table, yes, a safe table in Washington."

He closed the trunk, then placed a hand on Price's shoulder, his grip firm and steady. "Don't be a hero, Price. We need good men like you to come home. So be smart. Don't put your honor in front of a machine gun bullet—you won't win that battle. Just... be careful."

Price looked at his friend, at the crisp, new uniform and the extraordinary combination of ambition and fear in his eyes. He saw the path Reed had chosen, paved with connec-

tions and calculated moves, leading to a headquarters far
from the mud and the blood.

As Price turned to leave, he felt the burden of his assignment settle on him. His war would not be one of maps and
logistics. It would be something quite different.

47

THE GIFT

APRIL 1917

Charleston

The night before he was to ship out, they planned to meet in the hushed archive of the Charleston Library Society. The building was empty, the air thick with the scent of old paper and leather—a quiet tomb of silent stories.

Julia had left a side door unlocked for him. She stood waiting in the flickering light of King Street's gas lamps filtering through the tall arched windows. It felt like the last sane place on earth.

As the great clock in the hall struck ten, its chimes echoing in the stillness, she heard his familiar, hesitant footstep on the marble. He was a silhouette among the towering shelves, a soldier about to be consumed by a story far more terrible than any bound in these walls.

They didn't say much at first. The words felt small and inadequate against the looming reality of the war. He told her he was leaving, and she nodded, her eyes, which had always been so full of sharp, intellectual fire, now soft with a deep, aching sadness.

"I have something for you," she said, her voice a near whisper. She led him to an alcove where she had been working and picked up a palm-sized object from the table. It was a little book, bound in worn, dark leather, so old that the cover was smooth to the touch.

He took it, his fingers tracing the faded gold tooling. "What is it?"

"It's a book of hours. Fifteenth-century, maybe." she explained. "But that's not the part that matters." She opened it for him.

Inside, there were no words, only a series of exquisitely detailed illustrations. Each depicted a scene of a man, his face etched with pain and resolve, carrying a heavy wooden cross.

"The Stations of the Cross," Price murmured.

"Yes," Julia whispered. She looked up at him, her gaze direct and full of understanding. "Don't think of it as a prayer book, Price. Think of it as a story. A map. It's about a man who is judged, who carries an impossible burden, who falls, not once, but three times. But each time, he is helped, he is comforted, and he gets up again. He is stripped of everything he has, and is nailed to his duty."

She gently closed the book in his hands. "You are going to a place where you will see things that have no words. I want you to have this, not for faith in God, necessarily, but for faith in the human heart's ability to endure. Think of it as a map for a soldier's spirit. When you feel like you're falling, remember this map."

He looked at the book with the eyes of a soldier being sent off to war and made the connection—a map of endurance. The will of a soldier to fight, to get back up, to move forward, when all seems lost, is the key, he thought, like Grant at Shiloh. The gift was not just an act of grace; it was a strategy for survival.

He could find no words. He pulled her to him, his embrace desperate. "*À bientôt*," he whispered against her hair, the French words a fragile prayer. 'See you soon.'

He could feel her tears against his cheek as she held him tighter. "*Que Dieu te garde*," she choked out, her voice breaking. 'May God keep you.'

When he let go, he tucked the small book into the breast pocket of his new uniform—unconsciously close to his heart.

"Thank you," he said and left.

Julia's Journal

April 1917

He is gone. The library feels hollow tonight, the silence heavier than usual. I can still feel the imprint of his uniform against my cheek, the desperation in his embrace. To give a man a map for a journey through hell feels like such a small gesture against the machinery of war. I pray it is enough.

I did not say 'I love you.' The words felt too large for the moment, and too small for the truth. Love is not a word you say lightly to a man they are sending into the abyss; it is a promise you keep in your heart for his return. I have given him a story of endurance, but he has taken my heart with him as his shield. May it be strong enough. P.S. —I love him.

48

THE LONG WAIT

APRIL 1917 — APRIL 1918

America

W hen the United States declared war on April 6, 1917, America shifted on its axis. The hallowed grounds of the Citadel, once a crucible of academic discipline and tradition, transformed overnight into a veritable officer factory.

The year that followed was a war of its own—a battle against monotony in a succession of stateside training camps.

From the red dust of Fort Sill, Oklahoma, to the sprawling tent city of Camp Greene, North Carolina, where Price mastered the science of the French 75mm field gun and the military art of waiting.

In late March 1918, the orders for France finally came.

～

He had one last night. Clara met him in Charleston, and on a shared impulse, they took the ferry and the rattling trolley back to Sullivan's Island. It was where they had begun. It felt right to say goodbye there.

The island was quiet, the summer cottages shuttered for the season, the air cool and sharp with salt. They walked the beach, their shoes in their hands, the cold sand familiar and comforting.

They didn't talk about the war, or the year of training, or the future. They talked about the race, the first time they danced behind the carriage house, and the taste of the chicken salad sandwiches at their picnic. It was a sweet, desperate nostalgia, a grasping at a time that already felt like a distant, sun-drenched dream.

They found their way to the boneyard, the skeletal trees silver in the moonlight. Here, hidden from the world, the polite distance they had maintained in the city melted away. The reality that this was their last night, that he was leaving for a war he might not return from, was a palpable, unspoken thing between them.

Clara turned to him, her eyes shining in the dark. "I'm so proud of you, Price," she whispered, her voice thick with emotion. "But I am so, so scared."

"I'll be back," he said, the words a promise he wasn't sure the Germans would let him keep. "I'll come back to you."

"You better," she said, her voice a breaking whisper, and then she was in his arms. This was not the chaste, stolen kiss of their youth. This was a desperate, hungry embrace, a collision of two young people terrified of the future, clinging to the only solid thing in their world: each other.

It was the stolen dance, the study, and the picnic all rolled into one beautiful, aching moment. He tangled his hand in her hair; her lips were warm and soft, and the spark that had always been between them ignited into a roaring fire.

He was kissing her, really kissing her, and for a moment, the world of duty and war fell away. There was only this. And in that perfect, soaring moment, as he held her, he let the doubts of the past year—the staircases, the ambitions, the divergent paths—dissolve. There was only the salt on her skin and the desperate, undeniable truth of her in his arms. He held her, anchoring himself to this perfect, soaring moment, a memory he would carry into the fire.

The Charleston pier the next morning was a chaotic scene of steam, shouting, and tearful goodbyes. Price found his mother first, standing apart from the Chamberlains. She reached up, her hands fussing with the collar of his new officer's coat.

"It's too stiff," she said, her voice tight as she tried to force a smile. "You won't be comfortable."

"It's fine, Mama."

She stopped fussing and looked into his eyes, her own welling with tears she refused to let fall. "Don't be the hero they want you to be," she whispered fiercely. "Just be the good man your father raised. That's all. You just come home." She pressed his father's small, worn leather Bible into his hand. "It saw him through his trials. Let it see you through yours."

He couldn't speak, just pulled her into a hard, final hug.

When he turned, Clara was there with her father.

Colonel Chamberlain offered a firm handshake. "Do your duty, Lieutenant. We expect great things."

Clara's smile was a brittle, beautiful mask. The noise of the crowd was a wall between them. "Give them hell, Price," she said, her voice bright and public.

"I will," he promised.

For a moment, their eyes met, and in the space between them hung everything they couldn't say. She reached out, not for an embrace, but to straighten the lapel of his coat, a gesture of formal intimacy that ached with restraint. "Come back a victor," she said, her voice barely a whisper.

He nodded, the word landing with the weight of the world—a heavy anchor of expectation he knew he had to carry into the fray. Then he turned and boarded the troopship, the gangplank a bridge to another life.

As it pulled away from the dock, its horn blasting a mournful farewell, Price stood at the railing, watching the shores of America recede. He pulled the small Bible from his pocket. The leather was worn smooth.

He opened the cover and on the inside leaf, in the faded, elegant script of his grandfather, he saw an inscription:

To my son, on his ordination. May it be a compass in any storm.
1895.

He traced the words with his thumb, a connection to a line of men who had faced their own trials. The long wait was over.

He was sailing toward the storm.

PART III: THE STORM

"Nous Resterons Là" (We Shall Remain Here)

— Major General Joseph T. Dickman, Order to the 3rd Infantry Division, July 1918

49

ALL QUIET - PART I

MAY 1918

St. Nazaire, France

The transatlantic voyage ended not with the romantic skyline of Paris, but with the chaotic, rain-slicked docks of St. Nazaire. The air was thick with the foreign smells of coal smoke, brine, and roasting chicory.

Price, now a First Lieutenant in the 10th Field Artillery, stepped onto French soil and felt just like every other soldier: a world away from home. They were assigned to a training sector near Château-Thierry.

Life in this "quiet sector" was a jarring education in the realities of industrialized warfare. The trenches were not neat lines on diagrams, but claustrophobic ditches of mud, timber, and corrugated iron, teeming with rats and the constant damp chill of the Marne valley.

Here, Price was introduced to the men he would lead, a mix of hardened regulars and green draftees. Many of the fresh arrivals were still in their ill-fitting, olive-drab wool uniforms, their faces a mixture of boyish excitement and a deep, unspoken fear.

They carried the M1903 Springfield rifle, a weapon they had drilled with endlessly but had yet to fire in anger. Their gear was leaden, their packs loaded with everything from extra socks and a mess kit to a bayonet and a packet of letters from home.

His platoon sergeant was O'Malley, a stocky, 30-year-old Irishman from the steel mills of Pittsburgh with cynical eyes and hands hardened from wrestling hot metal. He also met Private Whitaker, a lanky, earnest farm boy from Iowa whose letters home spoke of missing the smell of plowed earth.

During an equipment inspection, Price found O'Malley wrestling with a French Chauchat machine gun, talking to it as if it were a stubborn mule. "Come on, you French devil. Don't be shy now."

He looked up at Price, wiping grease on his trousers. "Begging your pardon, LT, but I think the fella who designed this thing was paid by the Germans. You've got to hold it just right, whisper sweet nothings in its ear, and pray to a saint it doesn't spit its own guts out after two rounds. Give me a good old American shovel any day. At least you know it'll work when you need to hit someone."

He then patted the breech of a nearby field gun with grudging affection. "But this beauty... the 'French 75'... she's a sweetheart, this one. Sings a prettier tune than my mother-in-law, and she's a hell of a lot more accurate."

Price earned O'Malley's respect not in the command dugout, but in the horse lines. The French artillery horses were nervous, worn down by the constant, distant thunder of the front.

While other junior officers shouted, Price moved among

them with the competence learned at McCullough's Livery. He spoke to them in a low voice, his hands firm, calming a skittish draft horse with a gentle touch.

O'Malley watched his leader, unsmiling but with a flicker of approval.

During a lull, Price and O'Malley walked the line, inspecting a newly laid telephone wire that snaked through the shallow trench. A young Signal Corps private was anxiously tightening a connection on a field telephone set, a heavy wooden box with a hand-crank generator.

"Keep it buried deep, son, that's the only secure line to the front," O'Malley grunted, stopping beside them. "The first thing the Boche will aim for is this wire. A few well-placed shells, and we're as good as deaf, dumb and blind."

To which Price added jokingly, "And dead."

The private looked up, his face smudged with dirt. "We're laying three redundant lines, sir. But if the barrage is as bad as they say..."

He didn't need to finish. They all knew how fragile the connection to the guns was. A few strands of copper wire served as the lifeline, connecting the eyes at the front to the heavy artillery at the rear.

50

THE RIVER - PART II

JUNE 1918

The Marne River, France

I n June, as the 3rd Division settled into its role relieving
exhausted French units, Price was ordered to lead a
reconnaissance patrol. The mission was to chart
enemy machine-gun nests across a section of the river.

He chose O'Malley and a nervous but determined Private
Whitaker to accompany him. They moved under the cloak
of a moonless night, the air buzzing with the sounds of
insects and tension.

Whitaker, clutching his Springfield, moved with the
heavy-footed care of a man terrified of making a sound.
Price, however, moved like a hunter, his senses alive to the
terrain. He led them along a barely visible game trail, his
movements silent and sure.

They reached the riverbank, the water a black, silent
ribbon. Across the way, a German machine gunner, likely
bored and careless, lit a cigarette. The tiny orange ember was
a fatal mistake.

Price didn't fire; he marked the position on his map, his mind a cold, precise instrument. He saw two other nests, their positions given away by the faint silhouette of their water-cooled jackets against the skyline. It was enough.

On the way back, a German flare hissed into the sky, its ghostly green light washing over them and freezing them in place. They lay flat in the mud, hearts hammering, as a machine gun stitched a lazy pattern a few feet over their heads.

When darkness returned, Whitaker was shaking uncontrollably. Price put a steadying hand on his shoulder. "Breathe, son," he whispered, his voice calm. "Just breathe. We'll make it home."

He guided them back, not with commands, but with a confidence that quelled the boy's fear.

Back in the relative safety of their dugout, O'Malley met Price's eyes over a shared canteen of cold, tinny coffee. The sergeant gave a single, slow nod.

The bond, forged not in the heat of a great battle but in the shared terror of a night, was now unbreakable.

51

HOLD THE LINE
JULY 1918

The Marne River

By early July, the quiet sector was no longer quiet. Intelligence reports, confirmed by nervous French commanders, spoke of a massive German offensive —Operation Marneschutz-Reims.

The 3rd Division was tasked with holding a critical 7.5-mile front, a hinge in the Allied line.

Price's battery, the 10th Field Artillery, was positioned a few miles behind the front line. Still, the men dug in, their labor frantic under the summer sun.

As they prepared, Price found himself studying the terrain not for its beauty, but for its potential for life or death —the ravines that could hide an advance, the open wheat fields that would become kill zones, the gentle slopes that could offer some cover from the coming storm.

The men tended to the artillery, cleaned their rifles, wrote letters, and spoke in low tones of home, their gallows humor a thin shield against the palpable dread.

On a late afternoon, Price stood with Sergeant O'Malley on a rise, looking out over the placid Marne. The stillness was broken by the arrival of a French liaison officer, who made his way directly to Price, saluting sharply.

"Lieutenant," the Frenchman said, his voice a low, urgent whisper, his eyes wide with a fear that went beyond the usual strain of the front. "The intelligence is confirmed. General Ludendorff has stripped the Eastern Front bare. The collapse of Russia... it has given him a fearsome gift. They are calling it *Friedensturm*—the Peace Storm. A brutal piece of irony."

Price's jaw tightened. O'Malley just laughed, "Peace Storm? What's the objective? A piece of us?"

The French officer's eyes were grim. "Not a piece. All of you. All of us," he corrected. "He's moved nearly a million men. Fifty divisions. For the first time since 1914, they have more men on the ground than we do. They outnumber us, perhaps by as much as three to two."

The numbers settled over them, a suffocating blanket. This wasn't just another push.

"This is his *Kaiserschlacht*—his Emperor's Battle," the officer continued, his voice dropping even lower. "He's trying to win the war now, before your American legions can make a difference. Their objective is brutally simple: cross the Marne, shatter our lines, and march on Paris. They are within forty miles. If they break through here, the war is over. Not just for us." He gestured east, toward the capital. "For France."

It wasn't just a patch of riverbank they were defending. It was the last line of defense for Paris itself.

As the French officer departed to warn the next unit

down the line, an American runner arrived, his chest heaving as he handed a dispatch directly to Price.

The message was short, stark, and absolute. He read it once, then a second time, the words burning into his mind.

He turned to O'Malley and the other men who had gathered, their faces tight with anticipation.

"What's the word, sir?" O'Malley asked, his voice a low rumble.

Price held up the dispatch. "The order is from General Dickman" he said, his voice steady, betraying none of the cold dread he felt. He took a breath and read it aloud:

"'There will be no retreat. We Shall Remain Here.'"

A silence fell over the men. Private Whitaker, the farm boy from Iowa, swallowed hard and gripped his Springfield rifle until his knuckles were white.

"Remain here?" another soldier muttered, his voice barely audible. "He means die here."

Price's eyes locked onto the soldier's, his gaze hard as flint. "He means hold here," Price corrected, his voice cutting through the rising fear. "The General's given his order. We are the rock this wave breaks against. So dig in, say your prayers, and get ready to give them hell."

He folded the dispatch and tucked it into his pocket. He looked at O'Malley, then at Whitaker, then at each man in the circle. They met his gaze, and in their eyes, he saw the fear being slowly eclipsed by a grim, shared resolve.

The order wasn't just a command anymore; it was their mission, delivered by their officer. They would hold the line.

Price watched them as they began to check their ammunition and sight down the barrels of their rifles. He then turned his gaze back to the river. He thought of the leather-bound book in his breast pocket. His faith gave him some comfort.

The whole world was holding its breath. It was the same electric tension he'd felt on the beach at Sullivan's Island just before a summer squall.

He was ready for the storm.

52

TWO WORLDS

JULY 1918

The Western Front

The order to hold the line meant meticulous preparation, a constant battle against the flaws in their maps and the terrain itself. Price sat in the dim dugout light, Sergeant O'Malley watching him adjust coordinates on a mud-stained chart.

"Sir," O'Malley said, his voice a low rumble. "Begging your pardon, but you're not treating that map like holy scripture."

Price looked up, his finger tracing a contour line. "It's just a tool. I'm fixing it—checking it against the terrain—I've found some discrepancies. This ravine isn't marked, and there's a stone wall here that would give a machine gunner a perfect field of fire."

"My point exactly," O'Malley grunted, a flicker of respect in his eyes. "Most of the West Point shavetails we get, they're scared to even fold it wrong. They forget the map ain't the territory. You... you're listening to the ground. Studying. I seen you with the horses, too. You got a feel for things. That's worth more than all the trigonometry in the world out here."

Price just nodded, a silent acknowledgment passing between them. He shared his dwindling supply of American tobacco with O'Malley and Private Whitaker. "Back home," Whitaker said, "I used to curse the mud in spring planting. Never thought I'd miss that mud."

O'Malley chuckled darkly. "This isn't mud, lad. It's the Devil's ceiling. A mix of last year's crop, and generations of boys from places you've never heard of—a cap on the very heart of hell."

They laughed. And, for the briefest moment, Price felt less like a commander and more like one of the men.

That brief connection with his men felt real, grounded in the grim present. But the arrival of the mail sack, mud-splattered and smelling faintly of mildew, was a jarring intrusion from another life. His only remaining connection to the world beyond the trenches was through these fragile paper links.

Clara's letter was patriotic and beautiful, a portrait of the life he was duty-bound to lead. But he read it and felt a strange mixture of gratitude and guilt, as if he were failing to live up to the glorious narrative she was writing for him.

There was another package, a small, book-shaped parcel wrapped in brown paper. It was from the Charleston Library Society's "Books for Soldiers" program. He unwrapped it to find a slim volume of poetry by Alfred Tennyson.

Tucked inside the front cover was a simple, unsigned card in a familiar, elegant script:

Books for Soldiers

Mr. Hays,

I came across this and thought of our conversation on Shiloh. A reminder that even in the darkest trial, there is a harbor for the heart.

> "Tho' much is taken, much abides; and tho'
>   We are not now that strength which in old
>   days Moved earth and heaven, that which
>   we are, we are; One equal temper of
>   heroic hearts, Made weak by time and
>   fate, but strong in will To strive, to seek, to
>   find, and not to yield."
> —From Tennyson's "Ulysses"

Price read the lines, and then read them again. It was not a love letter. It was a message of understanding, a continuation of their conversation, sent across an ocean.

He carefully took the card from the book and tucked it into the same pocket as his small book of hours. It was a piece of a world he was fighting for.

For a moment, his gaze went to the small writing kit in his pack, the urge to answer almost overwhelming. But he let his hand fall. Some words could not be written. He could only hold onto them, a private sacrament in the mud, and keep his silence.

∾

Julia's Diary

June 1918

I sent the book. A foolish, hopeful gesture. I know he is an honorable man, who is spoken for by another. I expect no reply; to receive one would be a breach of the very integrity I so admire in him. But I cannot bear the thought of him facing that darkness alone. Let the words be a small light, a single candle in a vast and desolate church. Let him know he is not forgotten. That is all I ask.

Price tapped the book of hours, with the new card, in the pocket next to his heart. It had become a habit, giving him comfort, a fragile shield against the roar of the distant guns. His duty, the lives of his men, the memory of home—it was his cross to bear.

But his duties for the day were not yet done. He pulled a fresh sheet of stationery, the flimsy paper seeming wholly inadequate for the task ahead.

He had to write to the parents of Private Smith, the stocky boy from Utica. Smith had been killed two days prior, cut down by a machine-gun burst while laying communication wire.

Price could still see the boy's face, earnest and open, as he spoke of missing the apple orchards and cider of his home. He dipped his pen in the ink, but the words would not come. What could he say? Dear Mr. and Mrs. Smith, Your son died bravely.

The words were hollow, a tired platitude. He thought of telling them the truth: that their boy had died scared and in agony, calling for his mother. The ink bled from his pen onto the page, a dark, spreading stain.

He crumpled the paper in his fist.

Sergeant O'Malley, sensing his struggle, spoke from the shadows of the dugout, his voice a low rumble.

"Sir, if I may. Tell them he was a good soldier. Tell them his friends were with him. Tell them it was quick. Don't tell 'em how it really was. The truth of this place ain't for them."

Price looked at the veteran sergeant, whose eyes held a weary wisdom. He nodded, took a new sheet, and began to write, each word a carefully chosen stone, building a wall to shield a family in Upstate New York from the hell he inhabited.

The lies told from the front to the Homefront, he realized, were one of the heaviest burdens of command.

The days that followed brought a heightening tension to the front. Rumors moved faster than the supply trains—German divisions massing north of the river, pontoon bridges being assembled in the forests at night.

The quiet sector was holding its breath, waiting for the storm to break.

53

RED CROSS

JULY 1918

Charleston

The parlor of the Meeting Street matron had the scent of mothballs and old polished silver. The click of knitting needles was a nervous, incessant rhythm against a backdrop of venomous whispers disguised as patriotic concern.

Julia, her fingers methodically rolling bandages, felt a familiar sense of otherness—wondering who would be the unfortunate soul that would need the bandages, hopefully not Price.

The conversations were of Liberty Loan drives and the scandalous price of sugar, but beneath it all ran a current of suspicion. "Did you hear about the baker on King Street?" one woman murmured. "Gunther, I believe. They say he refuses to put patriotic posters in his window."

Another woman leaned in, her voice dropping. "My husband heard from a man at the port that German U-boats have been spotted off the coast of North Carolina. Can you imagine? The nerve."

Julia's hands stilled, the half-rolled bandage suddenly feeling like a funeral shroud. The whispers here were just a cruder echo of the silence she was now forced to police in her own sanctuary.

At the library, a government pamphlet, terse and clinical, sat fresh on her desk, instructing her on how to identify seditious conversations among patrons. A list of proscribed German authors had been circulated, their books deemed a contagion by association.

The war, she realized with sudden clarity, wasn't just being fought with bullets and bayonets; it was becoming a battle for thought itself, and her beloved library had been conscripted—turned into an intellectual front line.

That evening, after the last patron had gone, she ignored the order to take the volumes—Goethe, Schiller, Mann—to the furnace. Instead, she carried them to the deep, quiet archives of the library. There, among forgotten colonial shipping ledgers and dusty theological texts, she re-shelved them, hiding them in plain sight behind a row of Puritan sermons.

It was a small, silent act of treason against the new order; a promise that in her sanctuary, the stories would survive the war, even if the men who wrote them did not.

She thought of Price, facing a physical, honest enemy of flesh and steel. Here, the enemy was invisible, a poison of fear seeping into the very air. The clicking needles, the whispers, the space on the library shelf—it all converged.

This was her station: to sit and roll bandages, a small act that seemed insignificant to her, while a world away, the man who occupied her every thought prepared to face a war she was only beginning to understand.

54

THE U-BOAT

JULY 1918

Sullivan's Island

The summons came via a sputtering motorcycle courier from Fort Moultrie, a rare and urgent intrusion into the vigilance of the Coast Guard station. Colonel Chamberlain wanted to see Captain Adams immediately, and he was to bring his best man.

For Adams, that meant one person: Silas McGuire.

They found the Colonel on his broad, shaded porch, a place of polite society and gentle sea breezes that now felt charged with a grim tension. He wasn't in his customary wicker chair; he was pacing, a telegram clutched in his hand. He bypassed the usual pleasantries.

"Gentlemen," he began, his voice tight, "I've just received a priority dispatch from Naval Command. What we feared has happened. The Germans have brought the war to our doorstep."

He flattened the paper on a table, his finger jabbing at the text. "On July 2nd—an event they're already calling

'Black Sunday'—a single German U-boat, the *U-151*, staged a commerce-raiding spree sixty miles off the coast of New Jersey. In a matter of hours, it sank six unarmed American vessels. Used its deck guns, shelled them one by one."

A cold silence settled over the porch, broken only by the distant cry of a gull. Silas exchanged a look with Captain Adams. This was a different kind of war than the one they trained for. This wasn't about storms; it was about predators.

"The passenger steamer SS *Carolina* was among them," the Colonel continued, his eyes hard. "The German commander followed so-called 'cruiser rules.' He allowed the crews and passengers to take to the lifeboats before he sent the ships down. But in the chaos, one of the *Carolina's* lifeboats, overloaded with women and children, capsized in the dark. Thirteen souls lost."

The words hung in the humid air, a stark and terrible image. This wasn't a distant battle in France; it was American families drowning in American waters.

"Intelligence believes this is the start of a new campaign. These U-boats are now operating far south of the North Atlantic shipping lanes. They've hit North Carolina, and it is no longer a question of *if* they will reach our waters, but *when*," the Colonel said, his gaze locking first on Captain Adams, then on Silas.

"Your station is the only line of rescue for this part of the coast. Your orders are to maintain a 24-hour watch and be prepared to launch at a moment's notice. You are no longer just rescuing sailors from the weather; you may be pulling them from a field of fire. Do you understand?"

"We do, sir," Captain Adams said, his voice a low, steady rumble. "My men are ready."

As they walked away from the stately homes of Officers'

Row, Silas felt a shift in the world. The ocean, his old and respected adversary, was no longer a neutral force of nature.

It now held the malice of foreign men.

55

THE WATCH - PART II

JULY 1918

Sullivan's Island

The sign above the station door was different now. The old, weathered letters that had once read "U.S. Life-Saving Service" had been replaced by a crisper, more official sign: "U.S. Coast Guard."

The merger in 1915 brought regulations, new uniforms, and a new sense of purpose that felt heavier and sharper. The war had seen to that.

Silas McGuire, now a Chief Petty Officer, stood on the watchtower, his gaze sweeping the horizon. The summer haze shimmered over the Atlantic, a placid blue curtain that hid a terrifying danger in its depths.

The war in Europe, once a distant rumble, had arrived. Whispers and fragmented reports traveled down the coast like driftwood: German U-boats, brazen and deadly, were hunting off their shores. They called the waters off North Carolina "Torpedo Alley."

Down below, the station bustled with a nervous energy.

The former surfmen, now Coast Guard, a mix of grizzled islanders and raw recruits, went about their drills with a grim efficiency.

They were no longer just preparing for winter gales and stranded fishermen; they were preparing for war. Their motto had taken on a chilling new resonance.

"Anything, Silas?" a voice called from the ladder. It was young Burnham.

"Just the heat, kid," Silas replied, not taking his eyes off the sea. "And the waiting."

He thought of Price, somewhere in the mud and chaos of France. He'd received a letter a few weeks back, the paper-thin and smelling of damp earth and oil.

Price had written about the German artillery, calling it a "rip current of steel," a force that could pull a man under and never let him go. The words had resonated deep in Silas's soul.

He understood currents. He understood the unseen power that could drag a man to his death.

He scanned the horizon again, his eyes narrowed. Out there, somewhere beneath the waves, was another killer, a silent, patient enemy.

56

BASTILLE DAY - PART I

JULY 14, 1918

Charleston

The success of the Liberty Loan drives felt hollow as the casualty lists in the newspaper grew longer. The war was no longer an abstract cause to be championed from a stage; it was a tide of broken men returning home.

Driven by a need to do more, Clara volunteered as a nurse's aide at the naval hospital.

The reality of the hospital was a shock that stripped the world of its color. The romantic image of the handsome, wounded hero vanished, replaced by the grim truth.

The wards smelled of antiseptic, sweat, and the sweet odor of decay that clung to the back of her throat. The men she tended to were not the dashing officers from her father's parties. They were boys, their faces pale and etched with a horror she could not comprehend.

She saw men with missing limbs, their bodies irrevocably altered. She saw men whose lungs had been seared by mustard gas, their breathing a constant, shallow rasp.

But it was the ones with no visible wounds who haunted her most. The men with the "thousand-yard stare," whose eyes looked through her, fixed on a hell only they could see.

Men who flinched at the sound of a dropped tray, who screamed in their sleep, their minds shattered by what the doctors were beginning to call "shell shock."

One afternoon, she was tasked with helping a young soldier who had lost both legs below the knee. He couldn't have been older than Price. As she changed his dressings, he spoke, his voice a monotone whisper. "They'll give me a medal, you know. For valor. My mother will be proud."

He looked down at the space where his legs should have been. "The medal won't help me walk though." Clara held his hand and prayed with him, then finished her work in a daze, the soldier's words echoing in her mind.

That night, back in her pristine bedroom, Clara caught her reflection in the vanity mirror. She had expected to see a shattered, sorrowful girl. Instead, she saw a stranger, her eyes hard with a cold fury she had never known.

Her hands, resting on the polished wood, were not the delicate hands that had once held a tennis racket; they were hands that had cleaned wounds and held the hands of dying boys. A surge of righteous anger burned through her.

The polite battles of the parlor were a game. This—the suffering, the injustice—was real. She had once believed she could change the world from its parlors, but she knew now that the world truly only changes through its wounds. The girl her father had trained to smile through every slight was gone, and the woman who stood in her place had just found her war.

Heroism, she realized with a sickening clarity, was the price soldiers paid in blood and sanity, a debt that could never be repaid.

That night, she thought about the 4th of July letter she had written to Price, its pages filled with naive talk of victory balls and parades, and felt a flush of shame. She saw it for the fantasy it was. The polite world she was raised in was a fiction, and the brutal, honest horror of the hospital was the truth.

On this Bastille Day, in a ward of broken men, she had found her own liberation. This place of profound suffering had stripped her bare of her social pretenses. The debutante mill, with its parlors and performances, was a cage she would never return to.

She had found her True North. Her path would be public, impactful, and "ever upward." She would fight for these men, not in the shadows, but on the public stage. The girl who dreamed of debutante balls was gone, replaced by a woman who had found her purpose.

And as she thought of Price, her vision of their future shifted—away from the polite halls of Charleston society and toward the formidable halls of power in Washington, where the real decisions that saved or shattered these men were made.

She reached up, her fingers untying the silk ribbon at her throat, and left the knot on the table.

The sound was small, like a lock finding open.

57

THE INFERNO

JULY 1918

Offshore, Sullivan's Island

The call came just after dusk, a frantic crackle over the station's wireless. A passenger steamer, the St. Michael, bound for Charleston with forty-five civilians, had been torpedoed three miles offshore. Her last message was a desperate plea: "On fire... lifeboats damaged... sinking fast."

The seasoned men fell into disciplined action. "Launch the boats!" Captain Adams roared, his voice cutting through the humid night air. The Coast Guard crew, their faces grim in the lantern light, ran the heavy wooden surfboat down the ramp and into the churning surf.

The journey out was a brutal slam into the black waves. They smelled the wreck before they saw it: the acrid stench of burning oil and scorched metal. The scene that greeted them was an inferno on the water. The St. Michael was gone, leaving behind a spreading slick of burning oil.

Flames licked high into the air, casting a hellish light

over a string of chaotic, overcrowded lifeboats in the water, their occupants screaming. "Steer clear of the main fire!" Adams commanded, his eyes scanning the chaos.

"McGuire, rig the tow lines!" Suddenly, a sound cut through the din—the deep thump-thump of a deck gun. A German U-boat had surfaced on the far side of the wreckage, a sleek, black, dark shape in the firelight. A shell screamed overhead, exploding in the water fifty yards away, sending a geyser of spray into the air. They were being targeted. "They're firing on us!" young Burnham screamed.

"Hold steady!" Adams yelled over the roar. "They're trying to drive us off! Silas, get a line to that lead boat!" Silas was a fury, hauling the heavy tow line, his mind a steel trap of calculation. In the flickering light, he saw it—an overturned lifeboat at the end of the string, a mother and child clinging to its slick hull. The current was pulling them toward the heart of the burning oil.

"Captain! Aft of the last boat!" Silas shouted, pointing. Before Adams could give the order, Silas tied a line around his waist. "I'm going in! Give me fifty and pull when I signal!" He dove into the shockingly warm, oily water, swimming through the sludge. He reached the overturned boat, his hands finding purchase on the keel.

He saw the terror in the mother's eyes as she clutched her child. "Hold on!" he yelled. Suddenly, the world went white. A shell landed close, the concussion a physical blow that threw him from the boat. He surfaced, ears ringing, to see the U-boat turning its attention to them.

Captain Adams, seeing the immediate danger, made a decision. He was a father and a husband. He saw not sailors, but families. "Silas! I'm coming in!" Adams bellowed. Then, unbelievably, the Captain dove into the water himself, without a line. He reached the mother and child, shoving them towards Silas just as another shell hit the water nearby.

The blast wave caught the Captain, pulling him under. Silas saw his Captain's hand break the surface once, then vanish. He was gone. For a single, terrible moment, Silas felt a wave of despair so profound it threatened to pull him under—not again, not another one—then the child's scream, sharp and terrified, snapped him back to focus.

A wave of grief and shock washed over him, so powerful it almost drowned him. But the child in his arms was screaming. The mother was weeping. He felt the pull on the rope. He gave the signal. As he was hauled through the water, a single, fierce whisper escaped his lips, a promise to a ghost: "Not on my watch... this one's for you, Coste."

He was hauled back, dragging the survivors with him, his heart a cold, hard knot in his chest. As he was pulled aboard, he took command, his voice, when it came out, a raw, unfamiliar rasp. "I've got the tiller, Pull! Pull like you've never pulled before! Get us out of here! Now!"

The five remaining surfmen rowed with the strength of desperate men, their muscles straining as they began the impossible task of towing the entire string of lifeboats, escaping the kill zone as the U-boat finally submerged, leaving behind only fire and the dead.

58

THE LOST
JULY 1918

Sullivan's Island

They returned not as victors. The forty-two survivors they'd towed from the inferno were huddled in their lifeboats, their bodies shaking, their eyes vacant with a horror that would never leave them.

Silas, his face smeared with oil and grief, guided the lead surfboat through the last gentle breakers to the beach, the line of rescued boats following like a funeral procession.

The island had woken to the news. A crowd was gathered on the shore, their faces pale in the pre-dawn light. Women from the village rushed forward with blankets and hot coffee, their capable hands tending to the survivors with a compassion that needed no words as they were helped from their battered lifeboats.

Silas stumbled from the boat, the exhaustion hitting him. He saw Colonel Chamberlain standing at the edge of the crowd, his face a grim mask. Silas walked toward him, each step a monumental effort. "Chief McGuire," the Colonel said, his voice low. "Report."

"Forty-two survivors, sir," Silas said, his voice hollow. "Three lost from the steamer. The St. Michael is lost. Sunk by a German U-boat." He paused, the following words catching in his throat. "We lost Captain Adams. He went in after a woman and her child... he didn't come back up."

The Colonel closed his eyes for a moment, the news landing with a sickening force. He placed a hand on Silas's shoulder, a gesture not of an officer to an enlisted man, but of one man to another in a moment of shared loss. "He was a good man. A brave man."

"The best, sir," Silas whispered.

Later, after the survivors had been tended to and the terrible accounting was done, Silas stood alone by the boathouse, the adrenaline finally leaving him. A young surfman approached and offered him a tin cup of coffee.

As Silas reached for it, he saw that his hands were shaking, not from a chill, but from the delayed shock of realizing his friend and captain was gone. The tremor was an unwelcome stranger, a physical testament to the price of the rescue.

He looked back at the ocean, now calm and gray under the rising sun. It looked the same as it always had, yet everything was different. The war was no longer a headline in a newspaper or a letter from a distant friend. It was here. It had a cost. It had taken his captain, his mentor, his friend.

He thought of Price, on the other side of the same ocean.

59

BASTILLE DAY - PART II

JULY 14, 1918

The Western Front

On July 14, a strange and deceptive quiet settled over the front. In the villages behind the lines, faded French tricolors fluttered in the summer breeze for Bastille Day.

In Paris, there were fireworks. But in the trenches along the Marne, the silence was heavy, unnatural. The air itself felt thick with unspoken dread.

A young private from Georgia wrote a letter on a stained scrap of paper. "Dear Ma, it's beautiful here in its way. But tomorrow feels heavy in my bones. Like a storm you can't see but you can smell on the wind."

Across the river, under the cloak of that same unnerving quiet, German *Stosstruppen*—stormtroopers—were making their final preparations. Engineers moved like shadows, their hands sure and practiced as they assembled pontoon bridges, the sections locking into place with muffled clicks.

They were the vanguard of Crown Prince Wilhelm's last great gamble, the final push for Paris.

As the deceptive quiet of Bastille Day deepened into a tense twilight, the air itself felt full, coiled with dread. For weeks, there had been reports of German divisions massing north of the river and pontoon bridges being assembled in the forests at night. The German offensive was a palpable presence, waiting just across the rushing water.

As night began to fall, a final mail call brought one last letter from a world away. Price saw the handwriting on the envelope and his heart stopped—the same elegant, familiar script from the Tennyson card. But this was not a library parcel. This was not an official "Books for Soldiers" packet. This was a personal letter. He felt a sudden jolt.

A Letter from Miss Julia Moreau

My dearest Price,

The casualty lists in the paper grow longer each day, and my prayers grow more desperate. Forgive this intrusion, but I find I cannot remain silent. I think of you in that place, and I return to the map we once discussed.

When you feel you are falling, remember the Fifth Station: Simon helps carry the cross. It is a reminder that no man is asked to bear his burden entirely alone. There are those, even a world away, who would help carry the weight if they could.

When you feel you have been abandoned, remember the Sixth Station: Veronica offers a moment of comfort. It teaches that small acts of grace can be a fortress for the heart in a world of horror.

And when you feel you have fallen a third time, and can go on no longer, remember the Ninth Station. It is not the end. It is simply the station before you reach the summit.

You are a good and honorable man, Price Hays. Whatever trials you face, do not forget the path back to your home. That is the only victory that truly matters.

May God keep you,

Julia

He read the letter in the dim, flickering light of a dugout candle. Her words were not a plea for his love; they were a prayer for his soul.

He folded the letter and placed it with the card from Tennyson and the small book of hours. They were becoming the holy trinity of his survival, the tangible pieces of a faith he was clinging to before the abyss.

He thought of Clara's letters, full of pride and plans for the hero's return. They were letters for a man who was supposed to come home to parades. Julia's letters were for the man huddled in the mud, the man who might not come home at all.

~

Julia's Diary

July 1918

I have sent the letter. It felt like a sin and a prayer all at once. To write so plainly to a man who is not mine. But I see his face in my dreams, lost in the darkness, and I cannot stand by. I have offered him the only comfort I possess. Now, it is in God's hands. I have given him the map. I can only pray he finds his way home. If he returns to the life he is promised, I will keep my silence. My only hope is that the map I've offered him will help guide him to a safe harbor—wherever that may be.

60

THE CLEANERS

2000 HOURS, JULY 14, 1918

No Man's Land

Sergeant Michel Martin of the French IV Corps pressed his face into the wet mud of the trench parapet and listened.

The constant, distant rumble of supply trains, the faint but unmistakable vibrations of heavy guns being moved into position under cover of darkness—the signs were all there. The Boche were planning something big.

Tonight, his job was to steal their secrets.

"Ready, boys?" he whispered, his voice a low rasp. Around him, eleven shadows detached themselves from the deeper black of the trench. They were his raiding party, his *nettoyeurs*—the cleaners.

Their faces were blackened with cork, their hands taped around the handles of trench knives and weighted clubs. They carried no rifles, only pistols and a satchel of grenades. This was intimate work.

The plan was simple, which meant it was almost

certainly doomed to fail. Cross two hundred meters of cratered no-man's-land, cut through the German wire, drop into a listening post, and bring back a prisoner. Preferably one with a loose tongue.

"On my signal," Martin breathed. He waited for the next star shell to illuminate the landscape, its ghostly green light washing over a hellscape of shattered trees and muddy water.

As the flare died, plunging the world back into darkness, he gave the signal. One by one, they slithered over the top, becoming ghosts in a dead land.

The mud sucked at them, a cold, greedy mouth. They moved from crater to crater, the stench of rot and cordite thick in their nostrils. A machine gun opened up to their left, its tracers stitching a lazy, deadly pattern across the sky.

They froze, melting into the earth, their hearts hammering against their ribs. The gun fell silent. They moved again.

At the German wire, the real work began. With muffled cutters, they snipped at the barbs, the snap of the wire shockingly loud in the tense silence. It took an eternity.

Finally, they were through. The German trench was a dark, serrated gash just ahead. Martin could hear a low murmur of German voices, a cough.

He held up three fingers, then two, then one.

They erupted from the darkness in a single, fluid motion. Martin was the first one in, his club swinging in a silent, brutal arc. There was a sickening crunch, a muffled cry. The two German sentries never stood a chance.

As his men secured the dazed and terrified prisoners, Martin scanned the trench. It was a forward listening post, just as intelligence had predicted.

He grabbed a handful of papers from a small command dugout before his men began shoving their new prisoners back towards the wire. They had what they came for.

The return journey was a frantic scramble. Flares now lit the sky with terrifying regularity as the Germans realized what had happened. Machine guns opened up in earnest.

But luck, for once, was with them. They tumbled back into their trench, dragging five dazed and bleeding Germans with them.

They had the prisoners. Now they just had to make them talk.

61

ZERO HOUR

2300 HOURS

French IV Corps Headquarters (Rear)

The prisoners were a mix of sullen veterans and terrified young conscripts. They were separated and taken to a makeshift interrogation center in a reinforced cellar.

Lieutenant Arnaud, a young officer whose German was as fluent as his French, faced the first one—a boy who couldn't have been more than seventeen, his face pale with shock.

"The attack," Arnaud began, his voice calm, almost gentle. "When is it?"

The boy stared back, his eyes wide with a mixture of fear and defiance. He said nothing.

Arnaud sighed. He had no time for this. He gestured to a map on the table. "We know it's coming. Your comrades in the last raid told us it was planned for the 20th. Has that changed?"

It was a bluff, but a good one.

The boy's eyes flickered to the map, a tiny, almost imperceptible movement. But Arnaud saw it. He pressed on. "We know about the new guns. The extra ammunition trains. You cannot hide it. Tell me when, and perhaps you will see the sunrise from a comfortable camp, not a ditch."

He moved to the next prisoner, a grizzled *Feldwebel*—a sergeant—with cold, hard eyes. He got the same silence. But the prisoners were communicating with each other through their eyes, engaged in a silent, desperate debate. They were cut off, alone. Their duty to their Fatherland was crashing against their primal need to survive.

It was the fifth prisoner who broke. After hearing the lie that his comrades were already talking, he finally cracked. "After midnight," he stammered, the words tumbling out in a rush. "The rolling bombardment. It begins after midnight. The assault will be before dawn. Between three and five."

Arnaud felt a cold dread wash over him. He looked at his watch. It was 2330. They had thirty minutes.

The cellar erupted into controlled chaos. Runners were dispatched. Field telephones, their connections fragile and unreliable, crackled to life.

Arnaud got on the line to Corps headquarters himself, his voice sharp with urgency, relaying the intelligence. "The Friedensturm begins tonight. Bombardment at 0010. Waves of assault before 0300."

The message raced up the chain of command, a spark jumping from headquarters to headquarters. Within minutes, orders were being sent back.

62

THE SERGEANT

2340 HOURS

10th Field Artillery Horse Lines (Rear)

The world seemed to hold its breath, the only sounds the distant, mournful creak of a wagon wheel and the low whicker of a nervous horse. The air near the stable was thick with the scent of damp earth.

Colonel McAlexander had summoned Price, the 10th's Liaison Officer to the 38th Infantry, to his command post at the front. As he was preparing his horse, Sergeant O'Malley found him checking the harness.

The horse, sensing the storm to come, stamped its foot and tossed its head, its eyes wide and white in the gloom of the dugout. Price didn't flinch, speaking to it in a low, soothing tone, one hand stroking its neck with a practiced calm.

He could feel the animal's powerful heart hammering against his palm, a frantic drumbeat that matched his own.

O'Malley stood for a moment in the shadows of the

embankment. "She feels it," he said, nodding toward the animal. "They always know first."

"They are the most marvelous creatures on this earth," Price replied, his attention still on the horse.

"They are, sir—they are indeed." He paused and added, "But I prefer a woman." Price and O'Malley shared a brief laugh at the attempt at humor.

O'Malley continued. "Lieutenant... what's coming... it's gonna be bad. Worse than before. The men... they're scared. But they're watching you. They see you're not just some stuffed shirt playing soldier. They trust you."

He met Price's eyes in the gloom. "Whatever happens, sir, we'll follow you. Just thought you should know."

It wasn't a promise of victory or survival. It was a simple statement of loyalty, a gift from a veteran NCO to a young officer on the edge of the abyss.

It was the highest praise a soldier like O'Malley could give, and it landed with more weight than any medal.

"Thank you, Sergeant," Price said, his voice firm. "Get them ready."

He swung onto his horse, turning its head toward the front. The ride to Colonel McAlexander's dugout was only a few miles, but it felt like a journey to the very edge of the world.

63

THE STORM

2345 HOURS, JULY 14 - 0010 HOURS, JULY 15

The Marne River, The Front

At 2345 hours, the Allied artillery cannons spoke first. The French IV Corps' trench raid had been a success, and the intelligence ripped from their terrified prisoners gave the Allies a precious fifteen-minute head start.

The preemptive barrage thundered across the valley, a violent, desperate attempt to disrupt the German assembly. Then, at 0010, the German reply came, and it was a hurricane.

The world dissolved into a single, continuous roar. The air was filled not just with the shriek of cannons but with the low, terrifying *thump-thump* of massive mortars, the *Minenwerfer*, whose giant shells the men called "flying pigs."

Across the entire 74-mile Marne assault front, thousands of German artillery pieces opened up. This storm of steel orchestrated a barrage of high explosives, shrapnel, and a sickening saturation of gas that turned the earth into a quivering, tortured thing.

"Gas!" a soldier screamed, his voice muffled. "Smells like garlic!" The order came to mask up. Soldiers fumbled with their British Small Box Respirators, the rubberized masks clinging to their sweaty faces.

The glass eyepieces immediately began to fog, and the clumsy mouthpiece made it impossible to shout commands, reducing their world to a claustrophobic hell of ragged breathing.

For the men huddled in shallow trenches only two hundred yards from the Marne, it was an apocalypse. They clung to the shaking ground, the blasts so close they could feel the heat on their faces, their minds numb with terror.

The 10th Field Artillery

In the chaos, the carefully drawn lines began to fray. From their artillery observation post on a hill, Sergeant O'Malley had his field glasses trained on the battle raging below.

A German star-shell suddenly hissed into the sky, its ghostly green light washing over the landscape. "Sweet mother of Mary... take a look at this," O'Malley breathed, handing the glasses to Whitaker.

Whitaker put them to his eyes and saw it clearly in the star-shell's glare—the sudden, strangely orderly withdrawal of the French soldiers from the lines adjacent to the American infantry positions at the river.

The flanks of the American front were now completely exposed. O'Malley let out a low curse. "They're leaving our boys. We're the sacrifice."

In reality, it was a brutal piece of theater known only to

the generals; the front line was a designated 'sacrifice zone' of men meant to absorb the German storm.

But for the American soldiers holding that line, O'Malley's bitter observation felt like the gospel truth: it was abandonment. They were suddenly and terrifyingly alone.

Small groups of soldiers, isolated and surrounded, now had to fight in three directions at once, their sectors transformed into islands in a sea of fire.

In the villages behind the lines, the civilians who had not fled huddled in their cellars, listening to the approaching storm.

Just that morning, on Bastille Day, faded tricolors had fluttered in the summer breeze. Now, the air tasted of doom.

Women clutched children, while old men, veterans of 1870, listened with a grim, knowing silence. They could read the battle in the thunder of the guns, a language of terror they had never forgotten.

Down a by-road, a stream of haggard country people poured from the direction of the Marne, on their feet, the women carrying babies, old people bent under preposterous bundles—blankets, garden utensils, wheelbarrows filled to the brim.

64

THE LIVING WIRE

0120 HOURS, JULY 15, 1918

38th Regiment Command Dugout, Mézy Sector

The 38th Regiment command dugout was a claustrophobic pocket of Hell carved into the shaking earth. With every fresh detonation from the Germans' guns, dust and loose dirt sifted down from the timbered ceiling, hazing the frantic light of a single gas lantern and powdering the shoulders of the officers huddled within.

The continuous, deafening roar was a physical pressure that vibrated through the bones and rattled the teeth. The air was thick with the smell of sweat, damp earth, and something metallic and sharp, like ozone after a lightning strike. A tin pot of coffee, hours old, sat on a crate, its bitter, stale aroma a futile attempt at normalcy.

Just then, the door flap was thrown open and a French liaison officer, Lieutenant Dubois, stumbled in, out of breath, his uniform torn and his face bleeding from a fresh gash on his cheek.

He staggered to the map table and saluted. "Colonel McAlexander, Sir," he gasped, his voice tight with urgency. "It is as we feared. The French line on your flank has not bent; it has broken... here," he pointed a trembling finger at one spot on the map, "and here. And we appear to be facing the spearhead of the German assault. We've identified elements of the 10th and 36th Divisions in the initial wave—two of their best."

McAlexander absorbed the report, his face grim. He looked at the faces of his officers, then back at the map. "The intelligence from the Fourth Army was correct, then," he said, his voice a low, dangerous rumble. "Ludendorff has brought his legions from Russia."

Dubois nodded, his chest heaving. "They are everywhere, Colonel. It is not a push; it is a flood. All communication lines to the front are gone. Not just cut—vaporized. There is nothing left to splice. Just craters. Sir, we need artillery fire. Now."

Colonel McAlexander stopped, his gaze turning inward, staring at a point on the far wall of the dugout but seeing nothing. The only sound was the shuddering of the earth and the trickle of dirt from the timbers above. The silence stretched, heavy and suffocating.

An older Major, unnerved by the delay, leaned forward. "Colonel?"

McAlexander held up a hand, silencing him without looking, his mind racing through impossible options. More seconds passed, each one an eternity.

Finally, his eyes refocused, locking onto the faces of his men with a grim, heartbreaking finality. He had found the only path, and it was a terrible one.

"We need a living wire," he said, his voice low and

strained. "A man to carry coordinates from the front to the guns. A man on a horse."

The silence in the dugout was suddenly absolute. Men who had stared into the face of machine guns now stared at the floor, unable to meet their commander's gaze.

A courier. A lone horseman.

A target from another century sent into a hurricane of explosive earth and fire.

Every man there knew what it meant. It wasn't a mission. It was a death warrant.

Colonel McAlexander's gaze, heavy with the weight of command, swept the faces of his men. He looked away, his hand resting on the map table as if for support, a man searching for any other path. But there was none. His eyes finally settled on the one man in the dugout whose duty it was to be that wire. He looked directly at First Lieutenant Price Hays, his assigned Liaison Officer from the 10th Field Artillery.

He did not ask for a volunteer. He was giving an order.

"Lieutenant," McAlexander said, his voice dropping to a gravelly, mournful tone. "The lines are gone. We're blind. You're the new line. Get to the 10th. Establish the circuit."

Price met his commander's gaze. There was only the quiet, unflinching acceptance of his essential duty.

In that moment, Julia's words echoed in Price's mind, sharp and clear. *Every man is judged by someone... The First Station teaches that even Christ was condemned.*

He felt it now—the judgment of his commander, a sentence delivered by the impossible odds, the fact that they would be overrun by twenty thousand Germans if he failed. He felt judged already, his fate sealed the moment the first shell fell. The only question left was how he would walk the path.

Caked in dust, his face drawn with exhaustion, he did not offer a speech. He did not posture. He stood before his commander, the boy from the Upstate, the horseman, the cadet who had been judged and found his way.

"Yes, sir," he said.

The words were simple, yet they resonated with the force of a cannon shot.

Before McAlexander could respond, Price was at the map table, his eyes scanning the unforgiving lines of the terrain, the horseman in him searching for a path a foot soldier could not see.

Dubois moved to his side. "You have the courage of a Frenchman, Lieutenant," he said, his voice a low murmur of respect. He glanced at the map and continued: "But the roads are pre-sighted killing zones. Both the Paroy–Mézy road and the railway line are beaten zones."

"I can ride a trail," Price said, his voice tight with focus, "but I don't know the path."

Dubois's eyes sharpened with tactical knowledge. "I do," he said, his finger joining Price's on the map in a sudden alliance forged in desperation. "The Boche are confident. They watch the roads, the open fields. But here," he marked a spot, "a shallow saddle out of the Bois d'Aigremont."

"The Forest of the Sharp Mount," Price translated aloud, a flicker of his Citadel French surfacing.

Dubois looked up from the map, a brief, genuine smile cutting through the tension. "That explains it. You are a Frenchman." A short, humorless laugh was shared between them.

"Upstate, South Carolina," Price corrected, his brief smile vanishing as his focus returned to the map.

"Then you will appreciate the terrain," Dubois continued, his finger tracing the contours. "You can ride in the valley of that saddle. It will keep your silhouette below the skyline and give you cover."

His finger moved along a faint line. "That path leads along a hedgerow, a covered seam that will take you here," he traced a pencil along a thin blue line, "to an old irrigation canal—what the locals call an aqueduct. It's a man-made stream with raised earthen berms and small stone footbridges every few hundred yards. The path alongside it hugs the slope below the skyline, so you can ride in its shadow. In the barrage, ride the lee of the berms for cover; if the field opens up and they find your range, cut under the bridges. It will lead you beneath the railway and out to the river at Mézy-Moulins. It's your only chance to live."

Price's eyes lit with recognition. "A reverse-slope traverse," he murmured. "A ghost path."

The phrase landed like a touch of home. He felt a sudden, vivid rush of memory: the packed-sand trails of Sullivan's Island that wound invisible through the dunes, and his father's quiet voice: *Ghost paths, trails meant for those who refused to follow the obvious road.*

Price met Dubois's eyes, the French lieutenant seeing only tactical resolve, but Price saw something else: his entire upbringing—his father's inner map and Silas's rip current lesson—converging to draw a line on this French battlefield.

"Exactly," Dubois said, a quick grin flickering through the tension. "A trail for a rider who knows when to disappear."

"The ride back to the 10th will be a race through Hell. This path," he tapped the map, "is your safest way back to us." Dubois grabbed a protractor and a length of string from his map case, his movements swift and precise.

He laid the string on the map, his finger tracing the three legs of the journey. "From your guns south of the Bois d'Aigremont, back to us," he murmured, tracing the first leg. "Then you swing southeast to coordinate with our batteries," he traced the second, "and finally angle west-southwest back to your command post at the 10th to relay fresh targets."

He looked at the triangular path the string now formed on the map, a perfect geometric shape imposed over the chaotic terrain. A thoughtful, almost reverent look crossed his face. "A ten-to-twelve-mile triangular circuit," he said.

He tapped the three points of the triangle on the map. "In my faith, this shape is a symbol of the Holy Trinity. We call it the *Scutum Fidei*—the Shield of the Trinity."

He looked up at Price, his eyes hard with the grim reality of the calculation. "Darkness is your friend, but daylight and star-shells are your enemy. So much can change the timing."

He tapped the map again. "A fast, risky loop, with a quick observation at the front, might take seventy-five, maybe ninety minutes. But a typical circuit, with cautious movement, will be closer to two and a half, perhaps three hours."

His voice dropped lower. "And the worst case... the shelling pins you down, a horse is killed, you're forced into a long detour... you could be out there in the storm for the better part of the night."

He looked up at Price. "My new friend, you are not just carrying a message... you are carrying the lives of every man on this line in your hands." Then, in a near-whisper, he added in French, "May the Shield of the Trinity protect you this night."

McAlexander watched the two lieutenants hunched over

the map, a rapid-fire exchange of French and English, their fingers trying to trace a path of survival.

Where moments before there had been only a hopeless sacrifice, there was now a plan—a chance. The grim set of his jaw wasn't just resolve; it was the look of a commander committing his last asset to a gamble he now believed could actually be done.

As Price turned to prepare, Dubois snapped a salute to the Colonel. "Sir, with your permission, I will return to my lookout post. I must be there to receive him."

"Permission granted, Lieutenant," McAlexander said, returning the salute. "Godspeed."

Dubois gave Price a final, firm nod. "And now, I begin my run," he said, his voice tight with resolve. "See you on your return, ghost." With that, he disappeared into the darkness.

McAlexander turned back to Price. He gave a crisp, short salute to send him off. "You have your mission, Lieutenant. Get back safely to the 10th with this intelligence ASAP, and establish a circuit between them, the French batteries, and this dugout. Get our guns the coordinates so we can send those German bastards back to Hell."

As the canvas flap fell shut behind Hays, McAlexander turned from the frantic energy of his officers. His eyes remained on the map, but he no longer saw the tactical lines. He saw the single, desperate path he had just sent one young man to ride—a fragile thread of a life sent to mend a tear in the entire Allied front.

The weight of command settled on him—not the thrill of a bold maneuver, but the cold, quiet calculus of sacrifice. He had just condemned one man to almost certain death for the chance to save thousands.

He closed his eyes for a brief moment, the roar of the

barrage outside a distant echo to the silence of his decision. "Godspeed, son," he whispered to the empty doorway.

Price found his horse in a makeshift stable in a covered trench. The dark horse was a creature of fire and spirit that reminded him of Mercury, its intelligent eyes taking in the chaos with a nervous energy. The animal shivered under his touch.

Price offered him the last piece of an apple from his rations, murmuring in a low voice, swallowed by the approaching thunder. "We'll call you 'Traveler,'" he whispered, stroking the horse's warm, velvet nose. "Just a short journey, a hard run, and then we're done."

The horse nudged his hand, a silent pact made in the final moments of quiet before the storm. He saw in the animal's unwavering gaze not just fear, but a deep well of trust. It was a trust he knew he was about to betray.

His mission began not by riding into the storm, but by riding out of its very heart. He spurred his horse away from the inferno at the front as fast as he could—disregarding all of his and Dubois' carefully laid plans and routes—to get the intelligence back to the 10th Field Artillery.

65

THE HAMMER
0130 HOURS

30th Regiment Line, Jaulgonne Sector

On the south bank of the Marne, Colonel Edmund L. Butts lay flat behind the Paris-Metz railroad embankment, binoculars pressed to his eyes.

He was a hard man, a veteran of the Philippines, and he had deliberately disobeyed the spirit of the French command's orders. They wanted a defense "with one foot in the water."

Butts saw that for the death sentence it was. He had prepared a defense-in-depth, a killing ground with the river as its centerpiece.

Through the smoke and chemical haze, he saw them—a grim flotilla of canvas assault boats filled with elite German stormtroopers. "Hold your fire," he hissed to the runner beside him. "Pass it down. Not one shot until they are in the center."

The tension along the line was a palpable thing. He could feel the desperate urge in his men to open fire, to answer the hell of the barrage with their own. But the order held.

The German boats, gaining confidence from the silence, pushed into the main current. Closer. Closer. Butts could make out the flicker of a flamethrower nozzle, the glint of a machine gun barrel. They were halfway across now. Perfectly placed. Perfectly vulnerable.

"Now," he breathed. He didn't shout. He lifted a simple trench whistle to his lips and blew a single, sharp blast. The sound was thin, almost pathetic, against the roar of the guns, but it was the signal.

All along the embankment, the heavy water-cooled machine guns of the 9th Machine Gun Battalion opened up in a single, coordinated roar, their interlocking fire turning the river into a charnel house.

Seconds later, the sky ripped open as the guns of the 10th, 18th, and 76th Field Artillery—including Price's—unleashed hell on the pre-plotted coordinates, bracketing the crossing sites and tossing boats into the air like toys.

Colonel Butts had not waited for the storm to hit him; he had lured it into a trap.

But still, they came, wave after wave of Germans. Those who survived the crossing scrambled ashore. The fighting became a desperate, close-quarters brawl along the railway berm.

66

THE ROCK

0200 HOURS

38th Regiment Command Dugout, Mézy Sector

The neat lines and confident arrows Colonel Ulysses G. McAlexander had drawn on the map table just an hour before were now a meaningless fantasy.

The earth shook, and another runner stumbled into the dugout, his face a mask of dirt and terror. "Sir, the Boche are across the railway tracks—behind us! The French line... it's just gone!"

The textbook answer was simple: a fighting withdrawal to save the regiment from annihilation. But McAlexander's gut screamed a different truth as he stared at the chaos unfolding on the map.

To stand was to be destroyed. To retreat was to fail, to break the hinge of the entire Allied line and open a clear path to Paris.

His eyes closed for a brief, terrible moment. The tactical map was irrelevant. He was back in the West Point lecture hall, the lesson searing through him: Grant at Shiloh. The only thing that mattered was the will to endure. To retreat was to break the army's spirit.

He saw it then—a third option.

A desperate, insane gamble. He saw the line not as something to be held or abandoned, but as a weapon to be wielded. His fist hit the map table, a crack of thunder in the small space.

"We're not giving them a goddamn inch of this railway line," he roared, his voice raw with a terrible resolve. "Not one." A major stared at him, aghast. "Sir, they're enveloping us! We have to pull back!"

"No," McAlexander snarled, his finger stabbing the map. "No," he snarled. "We don't give them a goddamn inch."

He grabbed a grease pencil, and with a single, furious motion, he redrew their reality. He drew a deep, curved "U" on the map.

"This is what we are now," he roared, his voice raw with a terrible resolve. He traced the shape for his stunned officers. "The center battalion holds the railway line. They are the anchor. The bottom of the U. They do not move. They are the rock."

He stabbed the pencil at the two flanks. "The battalions on the ends will pull back, pivot, and face outward. We bend the line into a horseshoe. The open end will face our rear, and the curve—the thumb—will face the river. We will let them think they are surrounding us, and we will slaughter them from three sides."

The major's face went pale. "Sir, that's suicide! We'll be trapped!"

"We're already trapped, Major," McAlexander shot back, his eyes blazing. "This is how we fight our way out."

The order was given, a ripple of desperate commands sent out into the storm by every man who could still run.

McAlexander had no idea if it would work or if he had just condemned his entire regiment to death. He had forged the anvil. Now he needed the artillery to be the hammer. And for that, he needed a miracle on horseback.

67

THE RIDE

0125 HOURS

The Battlefield, between Mézy and Grèves Farm

The ghost path, the hedgerows, the careful reverse-slope traverse—the intricate plan he and Dubois had traced on the map dissolved into irrelevant fantasy the moment Price hit the saddle.

The intelligence he carried was a live coal in his mind: *twenty thousand German soldiers.* There was no time for ghosts. He needed to be lightning.

He spurred his horse out of the relative cover of a ravine near the dugout, not into the subtle shadows they had planned, but into the open, churning chaos. He abandoned the path for the simple, brutal geometry of a straight line.

The world was a strobing, deafening hell. Star-shells popped and hissed overhead, washing the landscape in a ghostly, searing white light that revealed a nightmare of splintered trees and men writhing in the mud. He rode through it, a lone, frantic silhouette.

He zig-zagged, not as a tactic, but as a pure, instinctual

reaction to the crump of incoming shells, yanking the horse left as a geyser of earth erupted on the right.

An image of another race, another horse, flashed in his mind—the sun-drenched dirt of Middle Street, the roar of the crowd, Clara's hopeful face at the finish line.

Here, there were no cheers, only the unending thunder of the guns. The faces he passed were frozen in the mud, their eyes wide and vacant. He galloped past a dead artillery team, their horse still hitched to the limber, its legs pointing stiffly at the sky.

Traveler was a creature of pure, terrified heart. It ran with a desperation that matched his, its breath coming in ragged, painful bursts.

Price could feel the animal's powerful lungs beginning to burn, the great heart hammering against his legs. He was killing him. The thought was a shard of ice in his gut, but he spurred him on, the lives of thousands weighing more than the life of one magnificent, brave animal.

He was no longer a horseman; he was a weapon, and the horse was his ammunition.

68

THE KEYSTONE

EARLY HOURS, JULY 15

Bois de Condé, 28th Division Sector

As the German stormtroopers swarmed across the Marne, isolated platoons at the front fired signal flares into the sky—brief, desperate bursts of color that silently communicated the overwhelming strength of the enemy advance before the positions were swallowed by the gray German tide.

Farther east, in the dense woods of the Bois de Condé, a platoon of Pennsylvanians from the 28th "Keystone" Division found themselves in a trap. Their French allies, holding the line beside them, had vanished in the darkness, abandoning them without a word.

The Germans of the 36th Infantry Division poured into the gap, surrounding them. The young Americans, many of whom had never seen combat, fought with a desperate ferocity.

When their ammunition ran low, they fought with bayonets and rifle butts. The woods echoed with the sounds of a desperate, hopeless struggle. They were overrun.

A handful of survivors, dazed and bleeding, eventually staggered back to the American lines. They brought with them the horrifying knowledge of what it meant to hold a position "to the last man."

In a damp, musty cellar that smelled of earth and stored root vegetables, an old woman clutched her rosary as shells shook the packed dirt above.

Beside her, her granddaughter slept fitfully, oblivious to the thunder. Through the cracks of the shuttered window, she saw the flash of fire against the night sky, a constant, strobing light that illuminated the terror of the world outside.

She whispered a prayer not in Latin but in the plain French of her childhood: "*Seigneur, protège-les*" Lord, protect them.

69

THE RIP - PART II

0147 HOURS

10th Field Artillery Command Post (Rear)

P rice rode into the relative sanctuary of the 10th Field Artillery's horse shelter, the horse's sides heaving and slick with sweat, its breath coming in ragged, steaming bursts.

Sergeant O'Malley materialized from the shadows, his face a mask of grim relief as he took the reins. "Mother of God, sir, we thought we'd lost you," O'Malley breathed, running a practiced hand down the horse's trembling flank. "This one's done."

Price slid from the saddle, his legs unsteady. "See that he gets a double ration of oats, Sergeant." He didn't wait for a reply, pushing through the canvas flap of the command dugout.

Inside, the air was thick with smoke and the rhythmic thunder of their guns firing. He delivered his report to the battery commander, his voice flat and devoid of emotion, a recitation of the apocalypse.

He handed over the mud-stained paper with the intelligence and the first set of coordinates. The commander's face went pale as he absorbed it. "You're our only link, Lieutenant. God Speed."

As the gunnery officers began shouting the new coordinates, Price found a crate in a corner, away from the frantic energy. For a fleeting moment, he was alone in the storm. His hand went to the small leather-bound book Julia had given him.

He didn't need to open it. Her voice echoed in his mind, a counterpoint to the impending storm outside. He remembered asking her once in the hushed sanctuary of the library, his voice low, "What happens when the falling doesn't stop? When there's no one there to help you up?"

He saw her face then, her expression a mixture of compassion and strength. "That is the Fourth Station," she had said, her voice a steady anchor. "Jesus meets His Mother. Imagine that moment. In the midst of the crowd, the jeers, the pain—he sees her face. She cannot take the cross from him. She cannot stop what is coming. But her presence, her love, is a comfort that gives him the strength to continue. It is a reminder that even in the darkest trial, love is a fortress."

In that terrifying moment, facing a mission he now knew was suicide, Price thought of Julia. He thought of his mother, her unwavering resilience, a bedrock in his life.

Their faces, his mother's love, became his fortress. He was not alone. That knowledge settled in his soul, a resolve that prepared him for the storm he was about to face.

0200 Hours

His next mount was a lean Anglo-Arab gelding on loan from the French cavalry—a breed known for its courage and stamina—fiery but sure-footed, his ears pinned flat against the storm. The horse shivered under him, nostrils wide with terror, but when Price pressed a steadying hand to his neck, the animal responded with a surge of desperate courage.

Instead of the roads, he navigated by the terrain itself, following the ghost-path he and Dubois had charted. He spurred the gelding out of the relative safety of the Bois d'Aigremont forest... before angling toward the level track of the aqueduct. He remembered what Dubois had said—the bridges came every few hundred yards; learn their timing, and live.

As a shell screamed close, he slid beneath the lip of a stone bridge, waited three heartbeats for the barrage to step past, and then took the angle across the next field. Not a map of fear, Julia's map for the spirit, he thought, and adjusted his course along the dark seam of the aqueduct.

His course was set for the Paris-Metz line, a destination that felt a world away. A nearby shell-burst threw a shower of sparks from a ruined cart, a flash that reminded him of the Sullivan's Island trolley, its electric wire snapping and hissing as it rumbled over the wooden trestle.

For a split second, the thunder of the guns was replaced by the familiar, humming rhythm of the trolley car, a sound of summer, of order, of a world where tracks led to a predictable destination.

The memory was a sharp, painful luxury, a glimpse of a life that felt a thousand years away. He pushed it down, focusing again on the deadly geometry of the battlefield.

The air itself was a weapon. The continuous roar was a physical pressure that vibrated through his bones, and each nearby blast was a concussive force that slammed into his chest, stealing the breath from his lungs.

The air smelled of cordite, churned earth, and a sharp, metallic scent. The Anglo-Arab fought the bit, its eyes wide with animal terror, but Price held it steady, his voice a low murmur, whispering reassurances it could not possibly hear over the din.

He was riding by sound, a terrifying symphony of destruction. He'd wait for the deafening crump of a German shell landing a few hundred yards away, and in that brief, earth-shaking moment, he'd spur the horse forward, its hooves pounding unheard against the ravaged soil, swallowed by the greater thunder of the barrage.

Suddenly, another German star-shell cracked overhead, the pop-hiss a serpent's breath in the sky. The lane turned to midday. The searing magnesium white light wasn't just bright; it was a physical weight, pressing down and turning the landscape into a ghostly, frozen photograph, exposing every detail of their vulnerability.

Price instinctively slid his boot from the stirrup and threw himself and his horse into the nearest roadside ditch, feeling a thousand unseen eyes on him from across the river. For twenty seconds, they were statues, Price calming the terrified animal as the light hissed above them.

The horse trembled violently, its muscles bunched like coiled springs, its breath coming in short, panicked snorts. When the flare guttered and darkness rushed back in, it was a sudden, smothering blanket, leaving phantom green spots dancing in his vision.

He scrambled back into the saddle, his movements

urgent but practiced, a creature of the night once more as a high-pitched whistle crescendoed into a deafening roar as another shell detonated not where he was, but where he was going.

The Germans weren't just bombarding; they were bracketing, predicting his path. He remembered Silas's lesson: *you don't fight the ocean's strength head-on; you use your head to get out of its way.*

The German gunners were intelligent; they would anticipate a straight line and lay fire where they thought he would go. His only chance was to be where they could not see him, or to move in a rhythm they could not predict.

Price came up with a new rule of the rip for the battlefield. When he found a covered channel—a sunken road or a deep ditch—he rode straight and hard for the river.

But in the open, he never gave them a straight line. He moved at angles to the current of the guns, using the brief, violent lulls between shell impacts to spur the horse across the dangerous gaps and find the next piece of cover.

It was a constant, fluid calculation—a rider reading the rhythms of a hellish sea. He galloped through geysers of exploding earth, a single thought searing through the terror: for his men to survive, the line must hold.

0245 Hours

He reached the Paris-Metz railroad embankment, dismounted, and led the horse through a low culvert that passed under the tracks, the only way to cross without being silhouetted against the sky.

On the other side, he scrambled into a shallow trench, which was less a fortification and more a ragged wound in the earth, smelling of mud and fear. Men huddled against its walls, their faces ghostly in the intermittent flashes of light.

He ran low toward a lieutenant whose face was a pale smudge of mud in the gloom. It was Dubois. The Frenchman's cynical expression vanished, replaced by a look of sheer, astonished relief.

A young soldier beside him stared at Price, his blue-gray uniform almost indistinguishable from the German field-gray in the dim, confusing light. "Mon Lieutenant, qui est-ce?" *my Lieutenant, who is that?* Dubois' face broke into a wide, fierce grin. He looked from his soldier to the American officer who had appeared from nowhere.

"The ghost of the Marne," he said, his voice filled with awe.

"My friend, the battle has shifted while you were gone. The 30th—our eastern flank—is buckling. They are about to be overrun. The French batteries are the only guns that can reach them and save them. You must go to them first. It is the priority now."

"Corporal!" Dubois barked. "Give the Lieutenant the latest enemy positions. Every boat, every pontoon bridge, every damn machine gun nest you've spotted." The Corporal handed Price a mud-stained sheet of paper.

"They are crossing in force here," Dubois said, his finger jabbing Price's map, "and here. Our 75s must hit these coordinates, or the 30th is lost. You are not just a messenger, Lieutenant. You are their eyes. You must make them see."

Price nodded, the new coordinates searing into his mind, and was off.

∾

Arriving at the French artillery position near the Bois de Condé, he found a scene of chaos. He located the battery commander, a grizzled captain, and shouted the coordinates over the din. The captain looked at him, skeptical of an American officer diverting his fire.

"These are not my targets!" the Frenchman yelled. "My targets are here!" Price grabbed the captain's arm. "Your targets have changed! The 30th Infantry is being overrun. Dubois sent me! You must fire these coordinates *now*!"

For a beat, the captain stared, then saw the authority in Price's eyes. He spun around and bellowed the new orders.

Price watched the gun crews scramble, traversing their guns to the new firing solution. He didn't wait to see them fire.

He wheeled the Anglo-Arab around for the mad dash back to the 10th, spurring the horse into a gallop and clearing the battery's position, plunging back into the open, shell-torn fields.

It was then that a high-pitched whistle crescendoed into a deafening roar, and the world went black. A German artillery shell detonated so close that the concussion ripped the air apart. The horse let out a single, terrifying scream—a sound of pure agony—as its body was flung sideways, collapsing in a horrific tangle of broken limbs and blood.

Price was thrown far, hitting the mud with a force that drove the air from his lungs. He felt a searing pain in his shoulder as the ground shuddered around him. For a stunned moment, he lay there, the First Station of his Calvary complete: he had been judged by the storm and condemned—but the line must hold.

0330 Hours

He scrambled to his feet, his ears ringing. He was skirting the southern edge of the Bois de Condé when a salvo of shells bracketed his path, forcing him to veer sharply into the woods for cover. It was there, among the splintered trees and pockets of lingering gas, that he ran into them.

Two figures materialized from the smoke. On the shoulder of the man leading the horse, Price could just make out the red Keystone patch of the 28th Division. On the horse slumped another private, his skin beginning to blister, his breathing the harrowing, rattling sound of lungs burned by mustard gas—his mask dangled from his neck, fouled and useless.

"You're a long way from Pennsylvania," Price said.

"Replacement, sir," the man with the mangled hand replied, his voice a hoarse whisper. "From the Adirondacks. Upstate New York."

He gestured with his good hand to his friend. "He needs to get to the aid station at Grèves Farm. If we can make it." He then asked, "Where you headed, sir?"

"The 10th Artillery, then back to the front. I need to find a horse," Price said, the words tasting like desperation. The private on the horse looked up, a terrible, rattling cough shaking his frame. "You a runner, sir?" he choked out. Price replied, "I am today."

Before anyone could speak, the private slid from the saddle. He stumbled, his legs barely holding him, and leaned heavily on his friend for support. "Then take her, sir," the private choked out.

Price looked at the animal, a sturdy, honest-faced Morgan, its eyes trusting even in the chaos.

"No," the other private whispered, trying to push him back toward the saddle. "You'll never make it on foot!"

"He has to hold the line," the gassed soldier insisted, his gaze locking on Price with a feverish intensity. "Take him, sir. And promise us you'll give them hell."

The sacrifice was absolute. The horse was this man's best chance of reaching aid before the mustard gas finished its work, and he was giving it up without a second's thought. Price looked from the horse's trusting eyes to the wounded gaze of the young private.

In that boy—caked in mud, breathing poison—he saw a spirit he recognized: a man with a good man's compass, acting not for glory but for decency. It was the same quiet honor that had made him whisper a promise to Traveler.

"I will," Price said, his voice thick with a vow he knew he had to keep. "I'll give them hell for you."

Price, still stunned by the selfless act, asked, "What's your name, son?" The private fought the wet cough before answering, his friend holding him steady. "Grey, sir."

Price swung into the saddle, the name echoing in his mind. He had fallen, and like Simon of Cyrene helping with the cross, this young soldier had shouldered the burden, offering him the means to continue.

This was the Fifth Station, Julia's voice reminded him. A stranger's help when all seems lost. A reminder that you do not walk the path alone. He had taken up his cross and rode on.

70

THE SACRIFICE

DAWN — MID-MORNING

The Battlefield

The honest Morgan lasted only a few trips. A burst of shrapnel vaporized its flank, and the horse went down in a chaotic ruin of flesh and bone, pinning Price's leg. He wrenched himself free, his knee screaming in protest.

As he did, grief, sharper than the physical pain, went through him. With the death of each horse came a sorrow he had not known was possible. He loved these animals, understood their spirits, and now he was leading them, one by one, to their slaughter.

0500 Hours (Dawn)

He was limping badly when two motorcycles skidded to a halt. Riding one was a grim-faced American Colonel. "Lieutenant, what in God's name are you doing on foot?"

"My horse was killed, sir. I'm carrying fire coordinates for the 38th."

The Colonel's eyes hardened. "Dismount, Corporal," he barked. "Give the Lieutenant your motorbike." He then locked eyes with Price. "You tell the guns that Colonel Butts of the 30th is holding the line, but we need that fire, and we need it now!"

Price mounted the motorcycle, gunned the engine, and sped off, the Colonel's resolve a fire in his veins. He had fallen a second time, and a commander's will had given him the strength to rise.

As morning came, the fight changed. The dim, confusing light that had blurred French and German uniforms turned to a revealing dawn. It revealed Price as a visible target to every German spotter and sniper.

The motorcycle died. A crater swallowed the front wheel and threw him. He landed in a ditch, his body a single, screaming nerve of pain.

On foot. Again.

The air was a thick, blinding soup. Black smoke from high-explosive shells, yellow-green clouds of chlorine, and white smoke from Allied screens.

Into an oily black cloud, acrid and choking... out into a ghostly white haze, eyes streaming, lungs on fire.

It was his only cover... He smelled the sickly sweet, garlic-like tang of mustard gas in the low ditches and craters, a promise of a blistering, drowning death.

The mask went on. The world became a claustrophobic hell of fogged glass and his ragged breathing.

Mid-Morning, July 15

A shape behind the smoke slowly resolved itself into a small, stone farmhouse, its roof half-caved in. In the lee of a crumbling wall, a family—an old man with a face like a weathered map, a woman, and a small, terrified girl—was frantically trying to hitch a single, sturdy Belgian draft horse to an overloaded cart.

The horse was their only hope of escaping the inferno. It was their entire world.

Price knew, with a certainty that felt like a physical sickness, what he had to ask them to do—and the cost of his request. He approached them, his hands praying. "*S'il vous plaît, Monsieur, Madame...*". Please, sir, madam...

The old man looked up, his eyes wide with a mixture of terror and suspicion. He positioned himself between Price and the horse, clutching the reins protectively. "*Non! Partez!*" he cried, waving a dismissive hand. No! Go away!

Price took another painful step forward, his gaze pleading. He pointed back toward the roar of the battle, then drew a line in the air toward Paris.

Speaking slowly, his French clear, he laid the truth before them. "There is no time to flee," he said, his voice thick with an honesty that cut through the thunder of the guns.

"The road is gone. *Les Boches...* they are breaking through. If we do not stop them here, at this river, they will not stop until Paris. Fleeing is not safety. It is a death sentence on a clogged road. Our only chance—your only chance—is to stop them now."

The old man stared at him, his face a mask of anguished incomprehension. He shook his head violently, muttering,

"*C'est tout ce que nous avons...* That's all we have. Our son, he died at Verdun. The horse is all we have left of our farm—of him."

But the woman's eyes never left Price's. She saw past the mud and the blood, past the uniform of a foreign soldier. She saw the unwavering conviction in his gaze, heard the brutal logic in his words.

She looked at her granddaughter, who was clinging to her skirt, and then at the fiery horizon. A grim, heartbreaking understanding settled on her face. The time for running was over. The time for fighting was here.

She placed a hand on her husband's arm. Her voice was firm. "*Écoute-le, mon mari.* Listen to him, my husband... Our son fought so we might live. Let his sacrifice mean something." She looked at Price and gave a single, sharp nod. With a choked sob, a sound of sacrifice, the old man surrendered the reins.

His hands were trembling, but his eyes, when they met Price's, were filled with a terrible fire. "Arrêtez-les ici," the old man whispered, his voice a raw command. "You stop them here."

Price looked from the old man's desperate, pleading face to the horse, then back again. This wasn't just a request; it was a sacrament, a transfer of the last of a family's hope and the memory of a fallen son. He gave a single, slow nod, accepting the crushing weight of the man's trust. "Oui, Monsieur," he said, his voice tight with emotion. "I will."

His gaze then fell upon the little girl, who was clutching her grandmother's skirt, her eyes wide with a fear no child should ever know. In her face, he saw the innocent future they were all fighting for. He fumbled in his pocket and found the small piece of hard candy he had saved from his rations, pressing it into her small, dirt-smudged hand. "Pour vous, mademoiselle," he whispered.

For you.

The old woman held a small, wooden canteen to his lips. "Buvez, mon petit soldat," she whispered. *Drink, my little soldier.* The water was a balm.

In her face, he saw a reflection of his mother, of Julia, of a humanity that refused to be extinguished. It was the face of Veronica from the Sixth Station, wiping away the blood and dust, offering a moment of pure grace in a world of horror.

Their kindness and sacrifice gave him the strength to continue.

He mounted the Belgian, its broad back and solid presence beneath him a contrast to the lithe cavalry mounts he had lost. This was not a creature of speed and grace, but of pure, unyielding strength, a workhorse of muscle and bone.

For a moment, he leaned forward, pressing his face against the horse's thick, warm neck, the simple, honest smell of the animal a grounding force in the madness. He was bruised, battered, and bleeding, but a fire had been lit in him, a resolve that burned.

The Ninth Station, Julia's voice reminded him. His third fall. He was stripped bare, his body broken, his mission on the verge of failure. And in the face of an impossible choice, a stranger's grace had helped him up again.

With a raw shout that was torn from his throat, a sound of both fury and prayer, he kicked his heels into the horse's massive flanks. The animal surged forward, not with a thoroughbred's speed but a locomotive's momentum, plunging them back into the storm.

～

The Belgian carried him for hours, a stubborn, unwavering force. He steered his panicked horse to the higher ground of the aqueduct line, using it as a track to spare his mount from the worst of the toxic vapor that pooled in the hollows below.

He galloped past a shattered stone wall where a faded advertisement for "Dubonnet" was still visible, a ghostly reminder of a peaceful world. In the distance, he saw the steeple of the church in Mézy, a landmark on his mental map, suddenly collapse in a silent puff of dust and debris.

He half-ran, half-stumbled into the trench, the familiar smell of cordite and wet earth now mixed with the metallic tang of fresh blood. He looked for the wry smile of Lieutenant Dubois.

He wasn't there.

A younger officer, a boy who looked no older than Private Whitaker, stared back at him, his face ashen, a somber red stain spreading across the shoulder of his wool uniform jacket.

"Where's Dubois?" Price yelled over the chatter of a nearby machine gun.

The boy just stared for a moment, his eyes hollow. "Took a mortar round, sir. Twenty minutes ago."

He didn't have to point. Price saw the row of still forms under the drab green ponchos.

A profound heartache settled in Price's soul. Dubois, his guide, his brief friend in this battle, was gone—just another poncho-draped body in a trench by the Marne.

There was no time for grief—but there was cold rage.

This was the Seventh Station. The loss of his companion, the man whose humor had been a small light in the darkness. He received the new coordinates—"Add 100; left 200; repeat"—and rode away alone.

Afternoon, July 15

The Belgian's strength could not outrun the Germans' storm. It died under a hail of machine-gun fire that tore through Price's thigh; the pain was a searing white-hot agony.

He dragged himself into a shell crater as German stormtroopers, shouting as they tried to cross the river, were cut down by the very artillery he had been directing. He could see the river was choked with debris, wreckage, and men.

The air was a cacophony of their cries, the wheeze of gas, and the drone of planes overhead. This time, there was no one. He was done.

He had failed.

71

THE FINAL FALL

AFTERNOON, JULY 15

No Man's Land, near Mézy

L ying in the crater, the world reduced to mud and the smell of his own blood, his mind drifted to Clara. He saw her as she was on their last night on the island, a beautiful, sun-drenched memory from a thousand years ago.

He felt the kiss, the desperate, warm embrace, the smell of salt in her hair... That was the promise. That was the life he was fighting to get back to. The wave of nostalgia, of love and passion, was a fortress against the pain.

But as he clutched the memory, it faded. The image of her on the beach dissolved, replaced by the image of her on the Hibernian Hall staircase—a beautiful, polished symbol of a world of performance and external validation. The wave broke.

He realized with sudden, devastating clarity that the man Clara loved—the 'victor' at her side on that staircase—was not, and could never be, him. The war hadn't broken him; it had simply burned away the last bit of him that could ever bow or perform for the sake of another's ambition, influence, or social position.

He was a man stripped bare. His Tenth Station. And he was, he realized, spiritually dying in this ditch. His trembling hand, acting on its own, went to his breast pocket. He pulled out the small, leather-bound book from Julia.

He thought of the story she had told him. The Empress Helena. The three crosses. The test on the dying woman. He laid both loves on the scale the way Helena had laid wood on the dying woman: the life of the staircase and the life of the harbor. Only one eased the break in him. Only one steadied his breath. Only one healed what was broken. And he saw the truth.

His love for Clara, the beautiful, passionate "wave" of his youth, the life of outward success—it was a love for the man he was supposed to be. It was one of "the other crosses." It was noble, it was real, but it held no power to heal the man he had become.

He looked at the book in his bloody hand. Julia's love. A love that spoke of falling and rising. A "map for a soldier's spirit," not a hero's parade. A map of true, enduring courage. A love that saw his vulnerability and called it strength. A love that offered grace, not expectation. This, he realized, was the "True Cross." The one that "heals what is broken."

The revelation brought no joy, only a profound sense of loss. To choose this path, to choose Julia, meant he had to kill the other part of himself—the part that had genuinely, passionately loved Clara. It was a betrayal, a rejection of a life he had *wanted* to be worthy of.

He was choosing to walk away from the high wave of his youth. The choice, he knew, would leave a scar deeper than any shrapnel. In that crater, his sense of duty to the staircase, to that type of ambition, had died. And in its place, his father's true current and Silas's parallel path became clear.

He saw his life not as a climb, but as a series of quiet, instinctive acts of service: the quarter returned so the maid wouldn't be docked; a shoulder under Silas's surfboat; a plunge into the rip for strangers; steadying Whitaker's rifle hand in the dark. In the market, he reached for an old woman's basket and met Julia's eyes; their fingers lifted together—a silent understanding.

These were the moments, he realized, not of glory, but of grace—each one a kept promise to his father on the Reedy, each a spark that warmed his heart and widened his soul. He saw his father's smile, his feet on the sandy shortcuts of Sullivan's Island. *Ghost paths,* his father had called them. A trail for a man who knows when to disappear. He finally understood. He wasn't a climber. He was a servant, a man of the library and the market, a man who belonged on the "ghost path"—helping others, unseen.

His promise to his father to be a good man, his promise to Private Grey to "give them hell," his promise to the old French couple to "stop them here"—it was all the same promise. A vow to serve, not to climb. That was his true north. That was his calling.

A new strength, born not of duty, not of ambition, but of this agonizing truth, surged through him. He made one final promise, this one to himself: if he survived, he would spend his life walking that ghost path, helping others find their way. He ripped strips of cloth from his shirt and tied them around his bleeding leg. Using a discarded rifle as a crutch, he began to move, one agonizing step at a time, back into the storm.

He had fallen again, but this time, he got up alone.

For the rest of that day, he carried coordinates and orders through a collapsed network of wires and shattered runners.

His route became a fluid calculation based on the locations of his fallen horses. The bodies of his mounts, once partners in his desperate mission, now served as grim landmarks of where not to ride, each one a testament to a path that had proven fatal.

Spotting the still form of the Morgan, he veered sharply, cutting through a ruined farm courtyard instead of the wild field where it had fallen. He found a tall, riderless Hanoverian, its movements rigid with the memory of a different army, its eyes wild with terror. He rode it until a line of machine-gun fire stitched across its chest, and it went down.

Scrambling free, he caught an Army remount, a skittish Thoroughbred cross whose lean frame was built for the racetrack, not the battlefield. He guided it through the chaos until a shell burst disintegrated the animal beneath him, the concussive blast throwing him forward into the mud.

His seventh and final horse was a heavy, broad-backed Percheron, a stubborn draft horse of immense strength meant for pulling cannons—a distant cousin to the steady animal that had once pulled his ice wagon—now tasked with a last, desperate race against death.

The ride was a blur of survival, and the desperate, forward motion propelled by the bond between man and horse—a refusal to yield to the impossible. The Percheron carried him for what felt like an eternity before a final artillery shell tore them both from the world.

He was thrown into a ditch, his body a canvas of pain.

As he lay there, next to his horse, he thought of its spirit... its unyielding will to fight for him, to move forward on the path, when all seemed lost.

His breakneck rides fed targeting coordinates to Allied artillery. The constant, accurate fire he directed allowed the Allies to break up the German pontoon boats and temporary bridges, shattering the enemy's attempt to cross the Marne in force.

By the evening of July 15, the Germans' attempt to force the Marne had failed. The 3rd Division held the line. The 38th Infantry, which had never given an inch of ground, had earned its immortal nickname: The Rock of the Marne.

Long after the German assault had broken down, Price was found beside his seventh dead horse, a bloodied, broken figure, unconscious, so still he was initially presumed dead like his once beautiful horse. He was taken down from the line of fire, his body shattered, but his spirit, finally, was whole.

He had faced the abyss and survived, and in the silence of his survival, the man he was meant to be was finally born. He was the vital link that allowed the Rock of the Marne to hold.

And, with a certainty that settled deep in his soul, he knew who he loved.

72

THE WARD
WEEKS LATER

A Field Hospital, France

The world returned in fragments. The sterile smell of antiseptic, the rough texture of a wool blanket, the low murmur of a doctor's voice speaking French to an orderly. For Price, consciousness was a minefield.

He would drift into a half-sleep only to be thrown back into hell by the imagined shriek of a dying horse or the sudden, visceral crump of an incoming shell. The pain in his leg, a deep, throbbing ache from shrapnel and shattered bone, was a dull distraction compared to the sharp, vivid horror of his memories.

He was a prisoner of the battle, trapped in a cot in a long, echoing hospital ward outside Paris. Days bled into weeks. He watched men with missing limbs learn to navigate their new reality. He listened to the quiet, desperate weeping in the night from men whose wounds were invisible, their minds utterly destroyed by what the doctors were calling "war neurosis."

He was one of the lucky ones. The surgeons had saved his leg, but the fever had nearly taken him. In the long hours of delirium, he rode again and again, the faces of the seven dead horses passing before his eyes. He'd wake up shouting, his hands clenched, the name "Traveler" a refrain on his lips.

A nurse, a kind, tired woman named Sister Agnès, would soothe his forehead with a cool cloth. "Reposez-vous," rest she would murmur. "La bataille est finie." The battle is over.

During the day, he would read. A volunteer brought him a stack of letters that had finally caught up to him. He read his mother's letter first. Her familiar script spoke of a deadly influenza sweeping through the Carolinas, a fear that reached him even in France.

It was a new kind of dread—a feeling of helplessness against an enemy he could not fight, a world away from his mother.

He read Clara's next. Her letter, smelling faintly of perfume, was a dispatch from another universe. Its bright, confident tone belonged to a world before the Marne, a world of 4th of July celebrations and plans for victory parades. She wrote of their life together, of taking their place in Washington.

The ambitious hero she was writing to, the man who could climb that staircase—that man was gone. He had died in the mud of the Marne, his duty to that type of ambition surrendered in a shell crater.

His gaze then fell to the two messages that had become

his anchors: the card from Julia with its quote on the will "to strive... and not to yield," and the small, worn book of hours. They were not a campaign strategy; they were a quiet harbor. He clung to them and to the path he had chosen.

He looked down at the small, worn book in his hands. He saw it now. His parents had taught him to serve: to follow the "compass" of decency. Silas had taught him to survive: to "swim parallel" to the world's deadly currents. And Julia... Julia had helped him endure: to find the map that gave him the strength to rise again.

One afternoon, Private Miller, a boy from Indiana in the next cot who had lost a leg at Belleau Wood, was crying softly into his pillow. Price, leaning heavily on his crutch, limped over to the boy's cot. "What is it, son?" Price asked.

Miller looked up, his face blotchy. "My girl... she wrote. She says... she says she's proud of me, calls me a hero. But she can't marry... this." He gestured to his empty pant leg. "She wants a whole man, like the one who left."

Price sat on the edge of the cot. He stayed there for a long time, his presence a quiet, steady anchor in the ward's sea of pain. He didn't offer empty platitudes. Instead, after a long silence, he spoke, his voice a low murmur. "A friend once told me a story," he began. "About an old empress who went looking for a ghost..."

He told the boy the story Julia had told him—of St. Helena, of digging for a truth the world had tried to bury. He spoke of the discovery of the three crosses, and how they tested them on a dying woman to find the one that held the power to heal.

The boy's tears stopped, his gaze captured by the ancient tale, a flicker of something other than pain lighting his eyes. Price leaned closer, his eyes locking with the boy's. "It's not a story about magic wood. It's a story about how you recognize what's real. My friend told me, 'The truth doesn't argue with you. It simply gives life. It heals what is broken.'"

He let the words settle in the quiet ward. "That girl of yours," he said, his voice gentle but firm. "Her love was like one of those other crosses. It didn't have the strength to heal. It couldn't see the truth. But that doesn't mean *you* are broken."

He gestured to the boy's chest. "What's in here—your heart, your courage—that's the True Cross, son. And one day, someone will come along who is dying for a little bit of that truth, and you will heal them just by being who you are. *That* is how you'll know."

"That's the map, son," Price whispered, his voice rough. "It's the story of a man who keeps getting up. I learned it in a crater. Lying alone. When everything went dark."

The boy stared at him, his expression slowly changing from one of despair to dawning wonder. For the first time in weeks, a flicker of something other than pain lit his eyes. Later that night, a nurse turned the boy's lamp down to a low glow. Price, watching Miller sleep, used his crutches to hop over and turned it back up, he said to the nurse. "He'll need it if he wakes."

Long after the ward had fallen into a fitful silence, the story Price had told remained with him. In giving the boy a map to find his own worth, he had finally read his own. He saw it with a clarity that was both a relief and an agony. Clara, with all her best intentions, partly loved the uniform—the hero who could win a place for them in the world. Her love was one of the other crosses.

But the man in this bed, the man who woke up screaming, who was haunted by seven dead horses and the faces of friends killed—the man forged in that fire could no longer walk her path. He would be a stranger to her.

Julia, however, had already met that man. He thought of her laugh in the market, a sound as real and uncomplicated as the sun. She hadn't offered him a future of victory parades; she had given him a light to survive the darkness. Her love was the one that healed what was broken. She wasn't waiting for a hero to return from the war. She was waiting for a survivor, a friend, to come home.

The choice, forged in the fire of the Marne—the test of the True Cross—was now irrevocably settled.

It was the splitting of his life: not a choice between two women, but between two men. One was the man he was supposed to be, beholden to a path of duty.

The other was the man forged by the fire, called back to his own soul.

PART IV: THE HARBOR

"We cannot direct the wind, but we can adjust the sails."

— Seneca

73

STORM WARRIORS - PART II

SEPTEMBER 1918

Written from Sullivan's Island, South Carolina

P rice,

I got your letter. Sounds like you are in a rip current bigger than I've ever seen. But you will swim it right. You've got salt.

I don't know if you heard, but we had a ship attacked by a U-boat, just past the breakwater. It was an inferno—oil and fire on the cold water.

We pulled forty-two survivors from the water that night. Lost three. You do the math, and it feels like a victory, but it doesn't feel that way when you're pulling a dead man from the waves.

This war... It's quite a different storm. It etches itself permanently into your memory, your soul.

You and I are a world apart, fighting different battles. But it feels like we're in the same boat, rowing together.

Just make sure you come back. The world will need good men to help rebuild it, and for the next rip current that comes.

Your friend,

Silas

Written From A Field Hospital, France

Dear Silas,

Your letter found me. It's a strange thing to say, but I was glad to hear of your hell. It makes me feel we were in this fight together, a little less alone with it.

You spoke of burning oil and cold water. Here, it is mud and hot steel. But we are in the same ocean.

When I was on that ride, the world was exploding. Shells crashing like the surf in a hurricane. I thought of your lesson on the beach. I couldn't fight it head-on. I chose my path to the front line, then followed the safest route back out, just as you taught me. It was like swimming parallel to the rip current. It helped save my life.

I see now that there are currents in everything. In war, in people, in your heart. You taught me how to see them. You taught me that you don't fight the ocean's power. You use your head to get out of its way.

It reminds me of your station's motto—about always having to go out, even when coming back isn't guaranteed.

Thank you for that. Stay safe.

Your friend,

Price

74

EXILE
SEPTEMBER 1918

Charleston

September did not bring relief. It brought a plague. The Spanish Influenza arrived in Charleston like a specter, slipping into homes, rich and poor, without distinction.

The city became a place of shuttered windows, muffled coughs, and the constant, mournful tolling of funeral bells. The library, once Julia's sanctuary, was closed by order of the health commissioner.

Driven by a need to do something, Julia volunteered as a nurse's aide at a makeshift infirmary set up in a converted hall at the College of Charleston. The scent of antiseptic failed to mask the smell of sickness and fear.

She spent her days bathing feverish foreheads and writing letters for the dying who, like Price, were far too young. One evening, after a brutal day where they had lost three patients, she returned home, bone-weary, to find her father struggling for breath, his face pale with fever.

The war, she realized with cold certainty, had more than one front.

Days later, her father was resting, the worst of the fever having broken. Julia sat by his bedside, re-reading a newspaper clipping she had carefully saved.

It was a small article from *The News & Courier*, detailing the recent recommendation for the Medal of Honor for a local hero, Capt. George P. Hays. The worn paper had become a fragile talisman.

Her mother, Helena, sat across the room, her hands stilled in her lap, her face etched with worry.

"He is a good man, this soldier of yours," Louis said, his voice a hoarse whisper. "I have read the report. The words speak of an honorable heart."

Julia looked up, surprised. "He is, Papa."

"He is also a Presbyterian," Helena said, stating the fact that hung in the air between them.

Louis sighed, a weary sound. "Hélène, please."

He turned his gaze back to Julia, his eyes full of a father's love and a deep, sorrowful understanding. "My beautiful girl, the war will end. This sickness will pass. And your young man, God willing, will come home. What then?"

The question was gentle, but it carried the world. Julia folded the clipping, her hands trembling slightly.

"I love him, Papa."

"But love is not the only current in this river." Louis said. "Your mother and I... we worry for your soul, Julia. You know what the Church asks of you. What it demands. To raise your children in the faith."

"What about his faith?," Julia countered, her voice soft but firm. "To deny his heritage, to stand aside while his children are raised in a faith that is not his own... that is a price I could not ask him to pay."

Her mother finally spoke, her voice laced with a pain that was sharper than any anger. "So you would choose this man over your faith? Over your family? Over God Himself? To be excommunicated, Julia... to be cast out? It is a spiritual death. I could not bear it."

"Mama, it is not a choice of him over God," Julia pleaded, her eyes welling with tears. "It is a choice to honor the man I love. Is that not a virtue? I cannot save my soul by destroying a piece of his."

A heartbroken silence filled the room.

Her father reached out and took her hand, his grip surprisingly strong. "You have your mother's fire," he whispered, "and your own unwavering heart. But the path you are choosing... it will be a lonely one. You will be an exile."

"I know," Julia whispered back, squeezing his hand.

"But I will not be alone."

Later that night, her heart aching with the terrible choice she had made before her parents, Julia's feet, acting on an instinct older than memory, carried her through the empty streets to the solid, reassuring presence of St. Mary's on Hasell Street.

She passed through the church graveyard, her fingers brushing the cool, weathered granite of old family tombstones, quiet testaments to endurance that gave her a small measure of strength.

Pushing through the heavy oak door, she dipped her fingers into the cool water of the font before making a reverent Sign of the Cross. She knelt in a familiar pew, the polished wood smooth beneath her trembling hands.

Her prayer was not elegant; it was a raw, desperate plea for her father, for Price, and for the strength to walk the path of exile she had chosen.

Her gaze drifted to the carved stations lining the walls, the map of suffering she knew so well.

It was the Fourth Station that held her: *Jesus meets His Mother*. In the sorrowful faces carved into the wood, she saw a truth that resonated deeper than her fear.

In Mary's face, she saw not divine sorrow, but a mother's unwavering love—a strength that did not remove the suffering but promised to endure it, a comfort that was a fortress for the soul.

She did not ask for a miracle to take the burden away. Kneeling in the solitude of the old Church, she prayed for the strength to become a comfort, not a burden, for her family, even if she might one day have to leave their world behind.

She rose from the pew, her burden no lighter, but her shoulders squared to bear it.

75

ALL QUIET - PART II
NOVEMBER 11, 1918

Charleston

The bells began to ring on the morning of November 11th. It started with a single, hesitant peal from St. Michael's, then another from St. Philip's, until the entire city of Charleston was awash in a joyous, clamoring symphony.

Julia, on her way back from an errand for her father, stopped on Broad Street, looking up at the sky as if the sound had a physical shape. People poured from shops and homes, their faces a mixture of disbelief and dawning, explosive joy.

A newsboy ran past, waving a copy of *The News & Courier*, the headline announcing Germany had signed the Armistice printed in letters so large they dwarfed the paper's masthead.

Strangers embraced in the street, tears streaming down their faces.

The city, which had held its breath through bond drives, through the grim tally of every son who died in uniform—1,987 from South Carolina alone—and the terrifying silence of the influenza quarantine, finally exhaled in a single, collective sob of relief.

Julia felt her tears come, hot and unstoppable—tears of gratitude for the end of the slaughter, and a desperate, fervent prayer that Price had survived to see this day.

The end had come at the eleventh hour of the eleventh day of the eleventh month, a poetic and sudden halt to the carnage.

The Armistice had been signed in a railway carriage in a forest in France, a strangely humble end to a war of such monstrous scale. The fighting had stopped.

But the silence that followed was a complicated one. The war was over, but the world remained at war. The men did not come home. Weeks bled into months, a prolonged, anxious limbo as the world's leaders gathered in France to forge a true and lasting peace.

For the soldiers in the field and the families waiting at home, the Armistice had ended the killing, but it had not yet finished the war.

The final, formal peace agreement was reached seven months later.

On June 28th, 1919, the Treaty of Versailles was signed in the glittering Hall of Mirrors at the old royal palace in France. It was an official, binding document, a line drawn in the ledger of history.

Yet when the news reached Charleston, there were no ringing bells, no dancing in the streets. There was only a solemn and weary acknowledgment.

And for Julia, and for millions just like her, a hope that this would finally bring the soldiers home.

76

HONOR
SUMMER 1919

Washington, D.C.

T he White House lawn was thick with sunlight, humidity, and the jubilant dull roar of celebration. Captain Price Hays stood in formation with a handful of men, his dress uniform crisp and pressed. Just moments before, the President himself had placed the simple blue ribbon of the Medal of Honor around his neck.

In the crowd of dignitaries and families, he saw his mother. She looked small and frail from this distance, her gloved hands clasped tightly in front of her. Their journey from the solemn grief of Greenville to this national stage felt like a passage through a hundred lifetimes.

General John J. Pershing, his face a granite mask of command, moved down the line behind the President. When he stopped in front of Price, the sheer force of the man's presence was palpable.

An aide read the citation, his voice clear and formal, "...First Lieutenant George P. Hays, 10th Field Artillery, 3rd

Division..." The words echoed in Price's mind. The *10th*. A number that had marked his trial and his salvation.

It felt less like a random assignment now and more like a station he had been destined to occupy. The aide continued, his voice a distant murmur, "...seven horses were shot under him and he was severely wounded..."

Pershing's eyes, which had seen the entirety of the war's brutal calculus, met Price's. "Captain Hays," he said, his voice a low rumble. "For conspicuous gallantry and intrepidity at the risk of your life above and beyond the call of duty... the United States of America thanks you." As was custom, he saluted Captain Hays, who saluted back.

After the ceremony, Price found his mother under the shade of a great magnolia tree. She reached out, her fingers tracing the star on his chest, her touch feather-light. "Your father would be so proud, George," she whispered, her voice thick with tears.

He looked at her face, truly seeing it for the first time in over a year. The lines around her eyes were deeper, etched by worry, but her gaze held the same unwavering strength he'd clung to his entire life. "It's heavy, Mama," he said, the words an admission of a burden he could not yet articulate.

She looked into his eyes then, and what she saw there— the ghosts of the Marne, the echo of the guns—made her eyes well up. This was not the boy who had left her. This was a man who had walked through the fire. She pulled him into an embrace, her shoulders shaking with quiet sobs of joy and relief, and he held on, burying his face in her shoulder.

He remembered how she had held him just like this after his father died, a small, fierce anchor in a world that had come apart. She had lost a husband to God's will; she had almost lost her son to man's folly. Her embrace held both the sorrow of that loss and the profound gratitude of his return.

"I'm thinking of staying in the Army," he said, the decision taking shape even as he spoke it. "When I see these recruits... they're so young. They don't know what's coming. Not the next war, but the one after that. The world doesn't stop. I think... I think I can help them. Teach them how to survive it."

She looked at him, at the unshakeable resolve in his gaze, and understood. He was no longer on the path they had dreamed for him. He was forging his own. "This is your station now, isn't it?" she said. "To be the one who marks the trail for them." She pulled him into an embrace. "Just be the good man he taught you to be. That is all I ask."

As they departed, Price watched a platoon of young soldiers drilling on a distant field, their movements earnest but clumsy. He saw their vulnerability, their raw courage, their terrifying innocence.

He thought of the seven horses, of Private Smith and all the others, of the terrible cost of being unprepared. His war wasn't over. It had just found a new front.

77

SERVICE

SUMMER 1919

Washington, D.C.

The ballroom of the Willard Hotel glittered, a galaxy of chandeliers and polished brass. Men in immaculate dress uniforms, their chests bright with ribbons, moved through the crowd with an air of practiced ease.

Price felt profoundly out of place. He walked with a slight limp, a permanent reminder of his time on the Marne.

"Hays! Price Hays, by God!"

Price turned to see a major approaching, his hand outstretched. It took a moment for him to recognize the face, fuller now, the eyes holding a new authority. It was Thomas Reed.

"Major Reed," Price said, shaking his hand. "Congratulations on the promotion."

"And you, Captain," Reed said, his eyes flicking to the medal on Price's chest. "Though 'congratulations' hardly seems the right word for that. I read the citation. A hell of a thing."

He gestured to a quieter corner. "Let me buy you a drink. We have some catching up to do."

They stood by a tall window overlooking the city, glasses of whiskey in hand. Reed spoke of his time on the General's staff, of logistics and strategy, of the smooth, efficient machinery of the war effort. He had been promoted twice, a rising star.

"And you?" Reed asked, his tone shifting, leaning forward with the intensity of a strategist. "You were there. At the Marne. What was it really like?"

Price looked past Reed, through the polished glass of the window, but he wasn't seeing the glittering city lights. He saw the flash of artillery over splintered trees, heard the whine of shells, and for a stark, terrible moment, he saw his friend Dubois, his face pale under a rain-soaked poncho where he'd fallen. He remembered Sergeant O'Malley's grim lesson, learned while censoring letters home: give the families a truth they can live with. The other truth, the real one, you must carry alone.

Price's focus returned to the room. He felt the phantom chill of the rain-soaked poncho. "It was... not quiet," he said finally, the words a shield built of O'Malley's wisdom.

Reed nodded, accepting the answer as sufficient data. He took a sip of his whiskey.

"That's the cost of entry, Price," Reed said, swirling the amber liquid in his glass. "But the accounts are settled. The world is under new management. And a man with your record, with *that* medal... you don't belong in a dusty training camp. You belong in Washington. I mean it. I can make one call, have you on a General's staff by Christmas. The real battles are fought here, in these rooms. We could climb the ladder together."

Price looked at Reed, at his immaculate uniform and his singular drive. Price saw it then—Reed's war was one of maps and reports, of calculated losses. He'd never had to kneel in the mud and hold the cost in his hands. The staircase was being offered to him, the highest rungs within his grasp.

"I think we have different mountains to climb from here, Tom," Price said, his voice quiet but clear.

Reed gave him that same shrewd, knowing look from the barracks years ago, the one that assessed every angle. "Speaking of which," he said, a genuine curiosity softening his expression. "Still caught in that same crossfire from before? Two girls waiting for you back home?"

A faint, sad smile touched Price's lips, a relic of a war he was finally leaving behind. "I no longer feel like a traitor, Tom," he said. "I've surrendered." He paused, his gaze turning back to the city lights, to a future he was finally ready to claim. "There's only one now. I just have to hope she's still waiting."

"Just one?" Reed's posture changed, the strategic lean gone, replaced by something more personal. A flicker of envy, sharp and quick, crossed his eyes. "Price, I've got no one. Sounds like you're one of the lucky ones."

Price thought of Julia, of her quiet strength, of the map she had given him when he was lost. "I hope so," he said. He extended his hand. "Thank you for the drink."

Reed took his hand, his grip firm. "Good luck, Captain."

"You too, Major," Price said, the difference in their ranks a simple fact, not a slight.

As Price walked away, his limp a steady, rhythmic counterpoint to the ballroom's distant music, he thought of Reed's words. And for the first time, with a certainty that settled deep in his bones, he knew they were true.

Yes, he thought to himself, a quiet peace washing over him. *I am one of the lucky ones.*

78

RETURN

SUMMER 1919

Sullivan's Island

The cheers in his honor felt distant, a sound from another world. His mind was a battlefield of memory. He saw the faces of the men who hadn't made it, the vacant, stony gaze of the ruined villages along the Marne.

War meant Death and disfigurement everywhere and to everything. He had been to the edge of the abyss, and the reflection he saw there would haunt him forever.

His hand went to his breast pocket, touching the small, worn leather book she had pressed into his hand—the illustrations of the Stations, a map for a journey he now more intimately understood.

He thought of Julia, her gifts and letters a lifeline in the mud, a reminder of a world where books and ideas still mattered. He had fought for that world, but he no longer knew if he could ever truly belong to it again.

He returned to Sullivan's Island a man transformed. The

Charleston *News & Courier* had announced his arrival, and his picture was featured above the fold:

LOCAL HERO, CAPT. HAYS, HONORED AT WHITE HOUSE

Pinned to the breast of his immaculate uniform was the simple blue ribbon and star of the Medal of Honor. As he walked down I'On Avenue, the familiar street felt alien. Officers on their porches, men who had once looked through him, now stood as he approached.

He saw Major Davies—the same man who had once called him "hired help"—snap to attention, his hand raised in a crisp, formal salute. It was not a gesture of friendship, but a symbol of respect owed to the medal, not the man.

Along the entire avenue, the gesture was repeated.

79

FAREWELL

SEPTEMBER 1919

Sullivan's Island

T he hot, salty breeze on Sullivan's Island was the same, but Price was different. Colonel Chamberlain was waiting for him on the porch, a place of memory, of summer breezes, of a beautiful dream Price had let go.

As he approached, the Colonel stood and began to salute. Out of a profound respect, Price's hand moved quicker, his salute snapping into place a fraction of a second before the Colonel's.

For a long moment, they held it, a silent exchange between two soldiers who understood the cost of duty.

Clara stood in the doorway, beautiful and poised, but with a quiet strength in her eyes. She didn't rush to him. Her gaze fell on the simple blue ribbon around his neck, on the star resting against his chest.

It was not a decoration; it was a scar made of metal and

silk, a physical barrier forged in a fire she could never truly understand, separating his world from hers.

"Captain Hays. Welcome back," the Colonel said finally, lowering his hand. "The entire nation is proud of you. We are proud of you."

"Thank you, sir," Price said. "I owe you a debt I can never repay. The opportunity you gave me..."

"You repaid it on the Marne," the Colonel said. "Now, I'll leave you two." He gave Price a firm, knowing look and disappeared inside, leaving them alone in the heat and afternoon humidity.

Clara stepped onto the porch. "I'm not wrong... am I?" she said, her gaze searching his. "The war... it changed you. I see it in your eyes. You're far, far away."

The words were a release. Price looked past her, toward the endless horizon of the Atlantic. "I am," he admitted, his voice hoarse. "The boy you knew... I think he died somewhere in the mud, between the screams and the silence."

He expected tears, a protest. Instead, he saw a deep, sorrowful understanding in her eyes that mirrored his own.

"I know," she whispered. "I met the men he died with at the hospital. The ones who stare at the wall and don't see it. The girl who wrote you letters about parades died there, too."

A sad smile touched Price's lips. "The future you wrote about, the life you imagined for us... It was a beautiful story, Clara. Everything a man is supposed to want."

"But that man isn't here anymore, is he?" she finished for him, the truth a quiet, shared ache between them. "By the time I found my way off the map my father drew for me, you had already found a different chart to follow, one that I now know is unknown to those who weren't over there."

A profound relief and an equally profound sadness washed over him. She understood.

"I've applied to Vassar," she said, her resolve clear as she looked out at the ocean, a very different woman. "I learned in that hospital that the world is broken in ways I never imagined. I intend to help fix it, not just watch it from a porch."

She paused. "I used to think of war as parades and brave young men in uniform. Now I know it's a debt paid in pieces of a soldier's soul."

Her maturity stunned him. The girl from the porch had fought her own war while he was away and won her victory.

"Our first summer here," she continued, a sad smile touching her lips, "it was a beautiful story, wasn't it? I must have written you a hundred letters in my head, all full of rebellion and stolen dances. But that girl... the one who was so thrilled to be defying her father... she's gone, too."

Price felt his throat tighten, a knot of sorrow for the two young people they had been, so full of hope and naive courage. In that moment, the love he had felt for her transformed into a deep, abiding respect.

He saw before him not the girl he was leaving, but a woman he would admire for the rest of his life. "You'll be brilliant," he said, and he meant it.

For the briefest second, Clara blinked, a quick, sharp motion to ward off a tear she would never let fall. She offered him a smile that didn't quite reach her eyes. This wasn't a break-up, he realized, but a mutual release. It was a eulogy for a love that had belonged to two people who no longer exist.

She extended her hand. Price took it, expecting the soft, delicate touch he remembered. Instead, her grip was firm, her palm steady. It was not the hand of a lover, but of an old friend.

"You will be brilliant too, George Price Hays," she replied, using his full name for the first and last time.

The Colonel reappeared as if on cue. A man of duty, he shook Price's hand. "You are a fine officer, Hays. A credit to the uniform. I wish you well."

Price nodded to them both, a final look of gratitude, and walked away. The weight of a life he couldn't lead was finally lifted from his shoulders, leaving only the scar.

80

AN OLD FRIEND

SEPTEMBER 1919

Sullivan's Island

He turned from the stately homes of I'On Avenue, but his feet did not carry him toward the trolley. He walked down the sandy lane toward the Middletons' stables. He needed a quiet place to let the world settle, a place that held no expectations.

The familiar scents of hay, sweat, and leather carried him back to Greenville, to McCullough's Livery, to the boy who had first learned that every horse had a spirit all its own.

Mercury was there in his stall, older now, the bay's muzzle silvered with gray. At the sound of Price's boots, the gelding lifted his head and let out a soft whicker, a sound of recognition that pierced Price deeper than any medal or salute.

"Hello, old friend," Price murmured, his voice thick with an emotion he couldn't name. He laid a hand against the horse's warm neck, feeling the steady, beating thrum of life beneath the hide.

Mercury pressed his head gently against Price's chest, the same gentle nudge he'd given on race day before thundering down Middle Street.

Price closed his eyes, the roar of the guns on the Marne a distant, terrible echo. He saw the others—the proud Anglo-Arab that leapt into fire, the honest Morgan, the captured Hanoverian. Seven companions, seven sacrifices, their last moments seared into his memory.

He stroked Mercury's withers, his voice a low whisper. "They carried me farther than any man deserved. And here you are... still carrying me."

The horse blew softly through his nostrils, as if in answer.

Price stood a long while in the sanctuary of the stall, his forehead resting against the gelding's warm, solid presence.

The war had taken so much, but here, in this simple, wordless bond, he felt a piece of himself returned.

81

A MESSAGE
SEPTEMBER 1919

Sullivan's Island

That evening, Price returned to the empty cottage. The emotional reunion with his mother and the quiet finality of his parting with Clara left him feeling hollowed out, as if he'd just completed one last, long march. He needed the ocean.

He walked into the surf, the cool Atlantic a shocking, welcome baptism. He dove through a breaking wave, letting the saltwater wash over him, a futile attempt to cleanse the grime of the Marne from his soul.

He floated on his back, and the conversation with Clara echoed in his mind—a respectful, kind farewell that had left him adrift. The life he had been building toward, the future she had planned for them, was gone.

He returned to the cottage and sat on the familiar porch steps. He picked up a piece of stationery.

He had to know.

Letter to Miss Moreau

Dear Julia,

I hope this letter finds you well. I find myself in a strange and unfamiliar country, not of mud and trenches, but of my own making. The path I thought I was on has come to an end, and I confess I am not sure of the trail forward.

I keep returning to a moment in the library, a lifetime ago. We were looking at an old map, and you said it was a fragile thing, easy to misread.

I fear I have misread everything. My map, my heart.

The war has stripped away so much, and in the silence that is left, I find myself thinking of your words, of the solace I found in our conversations.

I must ask you: Did I misread that map, too? Was the path of hope I felt between us only a line I drew for myself?

I will be in Charleston until the end of the week. Whatever your answer, I will be grateful for your honesty.

Yours,

Price

He sealed the envelope and sent it out into the world, a fragile message in a bottle cast into an uncertain sea.

82

A REPLY

SEPTEMBER 1919

Charleston

The letter arrived the next morning.

Julia saw the unfamiliar script and her heart gave a sudden, painful lurch. She took it to her room, her hands shaking as she broke the seal.

She read his words once, then a second time, a slow, radiant warmth spreading through her chest, chasing away the chill of the long months of silence.

He was not the brash hero from the newspapers; he was the man she remembered from the library—thoughtful, searching, and honest.

He had not misread the map. He had simply not known how to follow it.

She sat at her small writing desk, her reply brief and immediate. She would not confess the depth of her feelings on paper.

Some things had to be said face to face. Her response was not a declaration; it was an invitation.

Letter to Captain Hays

My dearest Price,

Maps are best read together. Meet me at the library tomorrow if you can.

Yours truly,

Julia

83

THE MAP

SEPTEMBER 1919

Charleston

The next morning, Price left the cottage.

He caught the first trolley, the car humming and sparking as it rattled over the long wooden bridge spanning the cove. He stood on the rocking ferry to Charleston, the salt spray cool on his face.

In Charleston, he didn't seek out a carriage. He walked. His limp, one of his many scars from the Marne, felt more pronounced on the city's cobblestones.

He walked past the grand houses South of Broad, with their wrought-iron gates. He passed the Hibernian Hall. He looked up at the grand, sweeping staircase, the one he had climbed with such awe, and later, with such a hollow, unsettled feeling. Now, looking at it from the street, a decorated hero, he felt nothing but a quiet relief that he would never have to climb those types of stairs again.

As he walked, one place called to him. Not a church, but a sanctuary of stone and silence, of stories and truth. The library. It was one of the only places he had ever felt truly seen. His steps, almost of their own accord, turned toward King Street. It was an instinctual pilgrimage.

Hope, a fragile, unfamiliar feeling, began to flicker within him again, followed by a wave of fear. The memory of their near-kiss in the archives replayed. He remembered pulling back; he thought he saw a flicker of hurt in her eyes before she said, "It's a fragile thing, a map... easy to misread."

Had he misread it?

Had he mistaken intellectual camaraderie and friendship for something more? Had he been summoned for a gentle rejection? The doubt was a cold counter-current to the fragile hope pulling him forward.

He stood at the bottom of the library's grand staircase, a mirror of the one at Hibernian Hall. But this one didn't feel like a performance or a climb. It felt like a hidden path to a cottage. It felt like home.

He reached the grand entrance at the top of the stairs and hesitated, his hand hovering over the large brass handle.

This was the final station. The end of a long, brutal road. He took a breath and pushed open the heavy oak doors.

The familiar, hallowed silence wrapped around him.

And then he saw her.

She was at a table near the tall arched windows, a pool of afternoon sun illuminating not a book but the single sheet of stationery he had sent her.

Her finger traced his words as though reading them aloud in silence—his message now a prayer between them.

She looked up, sensing his presence, her expression a mixture of curiosity and a dawning, impossible recognition.

The world stopped. The distance between them collapsed in a silent, profound acknowledgment. The smile that slowly, beautifully spread across her face was the only welcome home he had ever truly wanted.

He realized he was trembling; Julia was too. She rose from her chair, and in a few quick strides, they closed the distance and fell into each other's arms. Price's vision blurred as tears—hot, unchecked—spilled for the first time since the Marne, a release of all the grief and terror he had held inside.

He felt Julia's tears, warm against his neck, heard the small, choked sob that was a testament to her own long, silent vigil. It was not an embrace of passion, but of profound, bone-deep relief.

It was two survivors finding their harbor.

There were no questions, no need for explanations.

She had been waiting.

84

THE TENTH STATION - PART II
AUTUMN 1919

Sullivan's Island

That fall, they returned to Sullivan's Island.

They walked the beach hand in hand, the tide whispering against the sand, the wind carrying the scent of salt and memory. They stopped at the path to the Tenth Station—the place where his journey had begun. The ocean beyond the dunes was the same as it had always been, yet everything was different.

He looked into Julia's face and saw not just love, but the strength of a woman who had faced exile for him. And in his gaze, she saw the peace of a man who had ridden through fire and found his way back to her. Their silent, tear-filled embrace was a testament to the separate battles they had fought to stand together on this shore. The map had led them both through trial to this final, true station.

They walked on, their footprints side by side in the damp sand. Near the edge of the foam, something caught his eye— a glint of glass bobbing in the surf.

He waded out and lifted a weather-worn bottle, its cork miraculously intact. Inside lay a yellowed scrap of paper. He worked it free with care, the cork crumbling slightly beneath his thumb, releasing a faint scent of old paper and the sea. He unrolled the fragile note. The ink had faded, but he could still make out the words.

You have to go out, but you don't have to come back.
  — Silas

He stood for a long moment, the wind tugging at the paper, the waves breaking softly at his knees. Julia touched his arm. "What is it?"

"A lesson," he whispered, handing her the note. "From an old friend."

Julia read the words, a slow smile of wonder spreading across her face. She looked from the note to the vast, empty ocean, then back to Price. "Of all the bottles in the sea," she said, her voice filled with a soft awe. "This one finds its way to you, on this day. It seems some maps are drawn by a hand other than our own."

He looked from the weathered note to Julia's face, and in that moment, all the maps converged. He saw the path he had followed—a trail marked by the world's expectations: the uniform, the salutes, the medal. A rip current of earned glory that had nearly pulled him under.

But his father had taught him to feel the true current. Silas had taught him how to navigate it. And Julia... Julia had given him the chart for his spirit, showing him that the final station wasn't a summit of public honor, but a quiet harbor of grace.

He took her hand, the soft strength in her grip a familiar anchor. He was home now, in his harbor.

The sound of the waves was steady and rhythmic against the shore. It was no longer the roar of the guns, nor the chaos of the rip current. It was the sound of a heart.

Steady. Sure. Finally at peace.

He heard the Reedy River's patient rumble—the truth of the current he was meant to follow. He felt the ocean's hard lesson—the knowledge of how to swim the parallel path of his life. It was the Lesson of Currents, finally understood, and it brought a profound, quiet peace. It was a story of the hidden currents that lay beneath—a story of two men, and which one he would become.

A single porch light burned at the end of the lane—a light left on. On the porch rail, a small clear bottle caught the glow, a final sacrament, as if the river had finally, miraculously, delivered the lesson home.

THE TENTH SERIES

Light the Way for the Next Reader

In the vast sea of stories, a reader's review is a lighthouse. Your words can be the beacon that guides the next person to this shore.

If this story moved you, please consider leaving a review on Amazon. Even a single sentence helps honor the legacy of these soldiers and storm warriors.

Thank you for making this journey with me.

→ **Light the Way Here:**

Amazon.com

The Tenth Series

THE TENTH STATION (World War I — Standalone Prequel) 1918, France. Lieutenant George "Price" Hays makes a harrowing ride that earns him the Medal of Honor —but it is his choice between a colonel's daughter and a brilliant librarian that will define the man he becomes.

THE TENTH TRAIL MARK (World War II — The Climb) Twenty-seven years later, that officer—now a general—guides a new generation. Johnnie Grey faces the "unscalable" Riva Ridge, fighting not just for victory, but for the West Virginia farm girl whose silver cross he wears against his heart.

THE TENTH COMMAND (World War II — The Epic Conclusion) The trail ends here. As General Hays orders a desperate night attack to break the Gothic Line, Ranger Colonel Will Darby seeks atonement. Guided by Annie, a British codebreaker who sees the man behind the legend, they must close the gate—to bring their men home.

a amazon.com/dp/B0FXXR4MVW

g goodreads.com/joe_looby

THE TENTH TRAIL MARK

SUMMER 1927

Lake Placid, New York

The late sun shone across the Adirondacks, laying long bars of gold over the cabin yard. Grey sat on the porch, a shallow rasping cough snagging the quiet. The chill he brought home from the trenches never quite left him. He knew his time was short.

On the step below, four-year-old Johnnie watched. Nearby, his two-year-old sister, Allie, sat in the grass, methodically pulling petals from a flower. Between father and son lay a forked ash branch, a knife, and a square of sandpaper.

"All right, son," he said, voice rough. "Like this." He shaped Johnnie's small hands around the knife. "Slow. Feel the grain. You're not forcing it—you're showing the wood where to go."

A pale curl lifted from the ash. Then another. Father's hand over son's; the two of them worked patiently as the light slid down the yard. They sanded it smooth until the wood felt like it had always belonged in a hand. Leather pouch. Bands. A small click of knots drawn tight.

He set the finished slingshot in Johnnie's palms. "You made this," he said. "And it comes with a lesson. I learned it the hard way. The bravest thing isn't always fighting; sometimes it's helping."

He pressed a smooth stone into the boy's hand. "This teaches being still. Aiming true. Knowing the weight of one choice. That's a good man's compass, Johnnie. It's the only one you'll ever need."

Dusk gathered. Out in the yard, Johnnie propped a pinecone on the wood pile, pulled the bands back, and loosed. The shot went wide. He fetched another stone, set his feet, tried again.

From the porch, Grey's wife lifted Allie from the grass and settled her into Grey's weakened arms. They sat together and watched their boy. Pride and sorrow worked in Grey's chest as he watched Johnnie's stubborn stance. His wife rested her head on his shoulder, her gaze fixed on their son.

Johnnie sighted, breathed, and let the stone fly. In the last light, the pinecone trembled.

AUTHOR'S NOTE &
HISTORICAL CONTEXT

Author's Note

While the U.S. 3rd Division earned its immortal name as the "Rock of the Marne," the larger Second Battle of the Marne was an enormous Allied effort.

On July 18, the Allies launched a counterattack. In a massive counteroffensive near Soissons, American divisions marched through driving thunderstorms to reach their start lines.

At dawn, the attack began. French tanks, monstrous and loud, crawled forward, and behind them, the 1st and 2nd Divisions advanced, their objective the vital German-held rail hub.

The fighting was savage. Men veered off course in the confusion, regiments intermingled, but they pushed forward, taking villages like Missy-aux-Bois in brutal, close-quarters combat.

The momentum shifted. The Germans, their offensive

shattered, were now desperately defending. The fighting moved to places that would be seared into the memory of the American Expeditionary Forces.

At Croix Rouge Farm, the 42nd Division was ordered to take a complex of stone buildings that had been turned into a fortress.

The fight rolled on to the Ourcq River, where soldiers forded the water under fire, clearing machine-gun nests with hand grenades.

The 2nd Battalion, 166th Infantry stormed the town of Seringes-et-Nesles, a position as hardened as The Rock of Gibraltar.

The German line, hammered relentlessly, finally broke.

By July 22, the offensive had collapsed, and General Ludendorff authorized the evacuation of German forces—a decision that signaled the end of Germany's ambitions in the West. The retreat began, a slog through mud and shattered villages back to the Vesle River.

By August 6, the Marne salient had been eliminated. The threat to Paris was over. For the first time since March, the Allies held the initiative.

But for the soldiers who had held the line, there was no celebration, only the haunting memory of the blood that was shed. And the tally of the staggering cost. In three weeks of fighting across the salient, the American Expeditionary Forces (AEF) suffered nearly 40,000 casualties (killed, wounded, or missing in action).

The survivors were changed, hardened, and forever haunted. But they had held the line—for our security and freedom.

∽

Primary Historical Inspirations

While fictional, the spirit of the characters and the pivotal moments draw from real acts of courage and grace:

- **The Rock of the Marne (U.S. 3rd Infantry Division):** The Division's critical role in holding the line along the Marne River is a cornerstone of American military history. The heroic stand of its regiments, particularly the 38th Infantry, earned the Division its enduring nickname, "**The Rock of the Marne**".
- **Medal of Honor: George P. Hays:** The Medal of Honor citation for First Lieutenant George P. Hays forms the narrative spine for the novel's climax at the Marne. His mission—serving as the sole line of communication, having seven horses shot from under him, and continuing to direct artillery fire while severely wounded—is woven directly into the fictional journey of Price Hays.
- **The Tenth Station Rescue (Aquilla James Dyess):** The heroic civilian rescue at the novel's "Tenth Station" is modeled in spirit upon the real-life 1928 Carnegie Medal–winning rescue performed by Aquilla James Dyess on Sullivan's Island. This acknowledgment is intended to honor Dyess's unique legacy and his later heroism in World War II, for which he posthumously received the Medal of Honor.
- **Storm Warriors (Orleans Raid, 1918):** The historical U-boat attack and rescue known as the Orleans Raid of July 21, 1918—when surfmen

from the U.S. Life-Saving Service launched an unarmed boat under direct shellfire from the German submarine U-156 to rescue sailors from sinking vessels—provides the historical and spiritual basis for the U-boat attack off the Carolina coast. It also inspired the ethos of the novel's "storm warriors," embodied by Silas McGuire and the men of the Sullivan's Island Life-Saving Station.

∽

Medal of Honor Citation — George Price Hays

(Near Grèves Farm, France, July 14–15, 1918)

"At the very onset of the unprecedented artillery bombardment by the enemy, his line of communication was destroyed beyond repair. Despite the hazard attached to the mission of runner, he immediately set out to establish contact with the neighboring post of command and further establish liaison with French batteries, visiting their position so frequently that he was mainly responsible for the accurate fire therefrom. While thus engaged, seven horses were shot under him and he was severely wounded. His activity under most severe fire was an important factor in checking the advance of the enemy."

Source: Congressional Medal of Honor Society

Carnegie Medal Citation — Aquilla James Dyess

(Sullivan's Island, South Carolina, July 13, 1928)

"A. James Dyess helped to save Lucy W. Holley from

drowning, Sullivans Island, South Carolina, July 13, 1928. While Mrs. Holley, 24, was bathing in the Atlantic Ocean, she was carried by a current to a point 600 feet from shore. After several young men had failed to reach her, a woman swam to her and took her 20 feet toward shore. Dyess, 20, student, who was unaccustomed to swimming either in the ocean or for long distances, swam 420 feet through rough water to Mrs. Holley and the other woman. With great effort, Dyess and the other woman swam 400 feet with Mrs. Holley to wadable water."

Source: Carnegie Hero Fund Commission

ACKNOWLEDGMENTS

This journey has been profoundly shaped by those who marked the trail before me—teachers, mentors, and trailblazers whose wisdom and encouragement have consistently illuminated the rugged path. Though countless individuals deserve thanks, I wish to specifically honor a few whose guidance has been a particularly luminous beacon. Foremost among them is Nancy Looby, my mother, an unwavering inspiration and a radiant source of light in my life. The legacy of my father, Jim Looby, and his 10th Mountain Division brothers also forged an indelible and guiding mark on my spirit. My wife, Connie, and our children, Kate, Jack, and CJ, have always been a constant source of strength and joy. Our memorable visits to the shore, especially Kiawah Island, not only revealed the enduring beauty of South Carolina but also the profound bond of shared adventure and love. To my sister, my brother, and dear friends—your collective friendship has been a faithful and steady light. I owe special thanks to the historians, archivists, and veterans who helped bring this story to life. To the U.S. Army Center of Military History, the National Archives, and the countless researchers who document the lives of ordinary soldiers— thank you for keeping their voices alive. In particular, I'm indebted to Stephen C. McGeorge and Mason W. Watson; their foundational study, *The Marne, 15 July–6 August 1918*, informed and grounded these pages. My thanks also go to the "storm warriors" of the U.S. Life-Saving Service and the U.S. Coast Guard, whose legacy of courage helped chart the map beneath this story. Finally, to the veterans of the Great War, whose courage lit the trail for those who followed—your mark endures. To these remarkable individuals and groups—the "trail marks" on my life's ascent—and to the countless others, often unseen, who illuminated and guided my way forward, I offer my deepest, heartfelt thanks. With enduring gratitude for every step shared on this trail.

See you at the top!

ABOUT THE AUTHOR

Joe Looby, author of *The Tenth Station*, draws on a lifetime of ocean adventures and a legacy of military service to craft compelling historical narratives. An avid outdoorsman, U.S. Navy veteran, and Eagle Scout, Joe's work is profoundly inspired by his late father, Jim Looby, a 10th Mountain Division World War II veteran and recipient of the Bronze Star and Purple Heart. Through his series of novels, *The Tenth Series*, his company 10th Mountain Films, and acclaimed documentaries such as *The Year of the Tiger: JFK 1962* (2016), Joe brings history to life.

He resides near Charleston, SC, with his family, and gets to Sullivan's Island—a vital source of inspiration—as often as he can.

For the author's website:
TheTenthSeries.com

amazon.com/dp/B0FXXR4MVW
goodreads.com/joe_looby

www.ingramcontent.com/pod-product-compliance
Lightning Source LLC
Chambersburg PA
CBHW021407110726
47901CB00008B/2093